MOONSTONE

GEMS OF WOLFE ISLAND ONE

HELEN HARDT

MOONSTONE

GEMS OF WOLFE ISLAND ONE

Helen Hardt

Paperback ISBN: 978-1-952841-06-4

PRINTED IN THE UNITED STATES OF AMERICA

HARDT & SONS

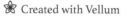

Created with Vellum

For all the Wolfes of Manhattan Fans!

ALSO BY HELEN HARDT

Calendar Boy

Daughters of the Prairie:

The Outlaw's Angel

Lessons of the Heart

Song of the Raven

Collections:

Destination Desire

Her Two Lovers

Non-Fiction:

got style?

PRAISE FOR HELEN HARDT

WOLFES OF MANHATTAN

"It's hot, it's intense, and the plot starts off thick and had me completely spellbound from page one."
    ~**The Sassy Nerd Blog**

"Helen Hardt...is a master at her craft."
    ~**K. Ogburn, Amazon**

"Move over Steel brothers... Rock is *everything!*"
    ~**Barbara Conklin-Jaros, Amazon**

"Helen has done it again. She winds you up and weaves a web of intrigue."
    ~**Vicki Smith, Amazon**

FOLLOW ME SERIES

"Hardt spins erotic gold..."

"Talon has hit my top five list...up there next to Jamie Fraser and Gideon Cross."

~*USA Today* **bestselling author Angel Payne**

"Talon and Jade's instant chemistry heats up the pages..."

~**RT Book Reviews**

"Sorry Christian and Gideon, there's a new heartthrob for you to contend with. Meet Talon. Talon Steel."

~**Booktopia**

"Such a beautiful torment—the waiting, the anticipation, the relief that only comes briefly before more questions arise, and the wait begins again... Check. Mate. Ms. Hardt..."

~**Bare Naked Words**

"Made my heart stop in my chest. Helen has given us such a heartbreakingly beautiful series."

~**Tina, Bookalicious Babes**

BLOOD BOND SAGA

"An enthralling and rousing vampire tale that will leave readers waiting for the sequel."

~**Kirkus Reviews**

"Dangerous and sexy. A new favorite!"

~*New York Times* **bestselling author Alyssa Day**

"A dark, intoxicating tale."

~**Library Journal**

"Helen dives into the paranormal world of vampires and makes it her own."

~**Tina, Bookalicious Babes**

"Throw out everything you know about vampires—except for that blood thirst we all love and lust after in these stunning heroes—and expect to be swept up in a sensual story that twists and turns in so many wonderfully jaw-dropping ways."

~**Angel Payne,** *USA Today* **bestselling author**

WARNING

The Gems of Wolfe Island series contains adult language and scenes, including flashbacks of physical and sexual abuse. Please take note.

PROLOGUE
KATELYN

P ain. Like sharp daggers digging into my shoulders.

One of them twisted both my arms so hard that both joints popped out of place.

Not enough that they've starved me, shaved my head, taken everything.

Now I'm in pain, and I'm going to die.

Die in this place. I don't know where I am. I don't care anymore.

Until I hear something. A shuffling. I curl into a fetal position, trying to ease the pain.

It doesn't help.

Still...someone is near, and whoever it is, the person is trying to be quiet, which means...

"Help me." My voice is soft, nearly inaudible.

More shuffling. Yes, someone's here. Someone who may be able to help me.

"Help me."

"Stop it," a voice—a female voice, thank goodness, says. "You're imagining things."

"I hear you," I say. "Help me. Please."

Perhaps I should feel relief, but I don't. What I feel is more like thankfulness that I'm not alone. For I will die here, and at least I'll have a companion. Maybe she'll hold my hand. Maybe she'll tell me it's okay.

Maybe she can get me out of here.

"Help me."

I see her then, her hand clasped to her mouth. She's blond, and she still has her hair. She's naked, as I am, and she has two slashes above her breasts that are oozing blood.

She kneels down next to me. "Hey. Who are you?"

"Please help me."

"Get up. Come on. Get up."

"I can't."

"You can. You have to." She shakes me gently.

I sob quietly as the pain rushes through me with her slightest touch. "That hurts."

"You can. Now get the hell up!" She grabs my shoulders.

"Aauuuggghhh!" I shriek as the pain surges my nerves into the very marrow of my bones. I'll die here. Alone. Unloved. Broken.

She lets go of me quickly. "What did they do to you?"

I swallow. "My shoulders. They're both dislocated."

"Damn. I'm so sorry."

"Can you pop them back in?" I eke out. Please. Please. Pop them back in. Help me. At least let me die without any more pain.

"I can't. I'm not a doctor. I might do more damage."

I close my eyes. She won't help. She won't even try. "Then please. Kill me."

She says nothing. Just stares at me.

"Please." I close my eyes. I can't look at her strong body. She

2

may have wounds, but she's still moving. She still has a chance. "I'd rather die here than have them torture me anymore. Please."

"I..."

I open my eyes, then. I'll make her look at me as she leaves me to die. "What's your name?"

"Zinnia. Like the flower."

"I'm Katelyn."

"Katelyn. I'm so sorry."

"Please, Zinnia."

"My friends call me Zee."

"Please, Zee."

"You can't ask this of me. How will I live with myself?"

I scoff softly. "Live with yourself? You won't live through this, Zee. You won't have to live with yourself for long." *She may be strong now, but they'll break her. They'll break her as they broke me. Maybe they'll dislocate her shoulders. Maybe they'll do something worse.*

"I'm so sorry," she says. "I'm not a killer."

I close my eyes once more, groaning. "Then run. I hear them coming."

She turns her head. "Maybe it's not them."

"It's always them. Now do as I tell you. Get the hell out of here." *I can't save myself, but I can at least try to give her a little more time.*

"I can't leave you."

"If you can't pop my shoulders back, and you're not willing to kill me, there's nothing more you can do."

"I can carry you."

"Then we'll both die."

She glances at me again and then over her shoulder.

Without another word, she flees.

And I wait for them to come kill me.

3

1

KATELYN

e hope you'll be happy here," Zee Wolfe says to me. She looks radiant with rosy cheeks and a pregnant belly, her honey blond hair pulled up into a messy bun.

Zee—Zinnia—whom I begged to end my life all those years ago, turned out to be my savior after all.

Now, finally, I'm thankful she refused to kill me that day. I want life—a life I have control over once more.

"I hope I will be also." I smile. It's a forced smile, but it's still a smile—something I once thought I'd never do again. "And Zee?"

"Yes?"

"Thank you."

"No need to thank me." She smiles, and hers isn't at all forced. "The Wolfes are happy to do whatever they can for you and the other women who were brutalized by their father."

Their father and countless others, I add in my mind.

But that's not what I'm thanking her for.

I pause a moment, as the images of the first time I met Zee emerge in my mind. I can't forget them. In a warped way, I don't want to.

"You okay?" Zee asks.

A loaded question. I'm not sure I'll ever be okay again. But I can live. Indeed, I *will* live. I'll adapt. I want to. I'm grateful to be alive. I'm grateful to have this new apartment in a building owned by the Wolfes. It's fully furnished with one bedroom and updated appliances throughout. Hardwood floors, too, which are shiny and gorgeous. I nearly slipped when we first got here.

"Do you have any questions?"

"No. Thank you."

"Don't forget"—she points to the emergency button by the door—"to use this at any time. For any reason."

I nod. She was very direct when she showed me the button by the front door and in the bedroom.

"We can always move you to a double," she says.

I shake my head. "I want to live alone. I need to."

"I understand. After six months at the retreat center, I'm sure you need some space."

Though the retreat center has nothing to do with my decision to request a single room in the Manhattan safehouse.

Zee doesn't call it a safehouse, of course. She calls it a furnished apartment, and it is. Except it's not. It's a safehouse —an apartment building the Wolfes maintain for the women who were rescued from Treasure Island.

I clear my throat. "How many women are here?"

"So far, just you, Aspen, and December. We're expecting another soon."

"Aspen?" December is Tigereye, but Aspen... Why does the name escape me?

"Garnet."

"Right. And I'm Katelyn."

"Only if you want to be. You can be whoever you want now."

"No, I'm Katelyn. I want to be Katelyn." I find myself affirming my name a lot. For a while, I nearly forgot it.

Some of the women at the retreat center chose to change their names, to truly begin a new life. I want to be Katelyn. Katelyn Mary Brooks from Los Angeles.

Katelyn Mary Brooks who visited Brooklyn one day in the past...and who never returned.

Except now I've returned.

"Whenever you're ready to contact your family—"

I gesture Zee to stop. "Not yet. I'm not ready to face them yet."

"There's no shame in what happened to you."

"I know that."

And I do. I'm not ashamed. I'm just...not ready to see my family for any extended period. My time with them wasn't pleasant. Of course, compared to my time on Treasure Island, it was fucking paradise.

Still...

"Are you sure you don't want the check-ins?"

I nod again. "I won't learn to walk again if I can't give up the crutches."

Honestly, it's bad enough I'm living in free housing provided by the Wolfe family, but I have no choice. Until I can find work and make some money, this is where I must live.

"You can always change your mind later," Zee says. "We have bodyguards available too."

A bodyguard is the ultimate crutch. No way.

"Thank you," is all I say.

"We've loaded the refrigerator and cupboards with food to last a few weeks. You can do your own shopping of course, or we—"

"Please." I hold up my hand. "I know you mean well, Zee. But I want to get out and take care of my own needs. I have to."

She smiles. "I understand. But if you change your mind—"

"I won't." My words come out more harshly than I mean them to.

"I understand," she says. "But tonight, dinner's on me. At The Glass House."

"Please—"

"I insist. Part of the program." She smiles weakly, but her blue eyes seem sad. "Let me do this for you, Katelyn."

I get it. Zee feels responsible for what I've been through. She's not responsible. Heck, if she'd done what I asked all those years ago, I wouldn't be here.

I nod and force another smile. "All right. A dinner. One dinner. And..."

"Yeah?"

"Thank you, Zee. For everything."

She reaches for my hand and squeezes it. "It is truly my pleasure. I just wish I could do more. I wish I could..." She shakes her head. "Well, you know what I wish. Call me anytime. Night or day."

I nod again. Neither of us has to say it. She wishes she could reverse everything that happened. To both of us.

I'll let her buy me dinner tonight, and I'll take her financial help for now because I have no other choice.

But I can't accept the bodyguard.

I can't have a babysitter any longer. I just can't.

I've always been determined to make it on my own, and even after living through hell, I haven't shaken that determination.

Except that one time.

That one time when I asked the woman standing next to me to end my life.

At the time, I thought I wanted to cease to exist—that no life at all was better than the pain and humiliation I was suffering.

Once I got to the island, though, I was glad I still had a life.

Even now, the thought seems odd to me, but I can't negate its truth.

I discovered something there. Certainly not freedom and certainly not peace. I was abused in the worst way, and I had to become someone else to get through it. I became Moonstone, and in some ways, I forgot Katelyn. I had to in order to survive.

But I found something I never knew I had.

I found strength.

And I found the will to live.

2

LUKE

Starting over is never easy.

Not that I'd know. This is my first time.

After three months of in-house therapy, I've been washed, wrung, and hung out to dry.

I'm a different person—in more ways than one.

Funny how things can change once you take the red pill.

And once you break away from those things that made you who you thought you were.

I hate New York. Always have, but this is where I am. Manhattan, a high-rise. I'm Luke Johnson—any man and every man.

I don't have to work, but I found that I wanted to, so I got a job waiting tables at The Glass House, an upscale eatery in Manhattan. I'm actually good at it. It was my work duty at the center. Who knew I had the sense of balance to carry two large trays—each filled with six full dinner plates—above my head without ever spilling a single thing?

That's talent, for sure.

I roll my eyes.

But hey, it's something to do.

Table fourteen is a two-top in my station. Two gorgeous blond women. I recognize one right away—Zee Wolfe, wife to billionaire Reid Wolfe of Wolfe Enterprises, and very pregnant. Means a good tip.

The other is— I widen my eyes to get a better look.

She's blond also, and even more beautiful than her companion. I'm usually attracted to dark-haired women, but maybe my attitude isn't all that's changed.

This woman, with her blond waves settling around her shoulders, attracts me like a magnet.

I'm not sure what it is about her, but it's more than her angelic face and milky skin.

It's her eyes.

They're big and blue and beautiful, but they're also... something else. Not sad, exactly. Just...resigned.

Those eyes have seen things. And not good things.

The two women are quiet, so I clear my throat. They look up.

"Good evening, ladies. I'm Luke and I'll be your server this evening. Would you care to order a cocktail?"

"Nothing for me." Zee points to her belly. "Just water is fine.

"All right, Mrs. Wolfe."

"You know me?"

"Of course. It's a pleasure to have you here." I turn to her companion. "And you, lovely lady?

The words popped out before I could stop them. But I'm not sorry. The blush on her creamy cheeks is worth it.

"Just water is fine," she says without looking up.

"Sparkling or tap?"

"Tap, please."

"Very well. Do you have any questions about the menu?"

Zee smiles. "I don't. Katelyn?"

Katelyn. She has a name. A beautiful name. It fits her. Katelyn.

"No." Katelyn stares at the nails on her right hand. They're short, unpainted. Not ostentatious at all, this one.

"I can tell you about our chef's specials, or are you interested in an appetizer?"

Zee smiles. "I think we need a minute, Luke, if that's all right."

"Of course. I'll get your waters." I smile and walk away.

I won't get the waters. The busboy will, which is fine.

Travis Stone, the server who trained me recently, grabs my arm. "Lucky you. That's Mrs. Reid Wolfe."

"Yeah, I know."

"Big tip coming your way. Who's that with her? She's even hotter than all the Wolfe wives."

Katelyn. I open my mouth to say her name and then think better of it. "I don't know. A friend of hers, I guess."

For some reason, telling Travis Katelyn's name feels all wrong to me. I have no idea why.

"You want to trade tables?" Travis asks. "I'll give you half the tip plus two of my tables."

Right. I don't think so. I'm not letting Travis anywhere near Katelyn. The man has one thing on his mind at all times, and it's not usually his work. He's a damned good waiter, but more often than not he goes home with one of his customers.

He's not going home with Katelyn.

Neither am I, of course. I'm not there yet.

But no one else is going home with her either.

"No thanks," I say, trying to sound jovial. "I'm not giving up a Wolfe tip."

Travis nods. "Can't blame you. Let's hope they order the Beluga caviar, dude. Can't beat starting with a five hundred dollar app."

"Not likely. No cocktails. Just tap water. I doubt they'll be running up a huge bill."

"Ha! Glad you decided not to swap, then. Though I wouldn't mind a shot at Ms. Wolfe's friend."

Warmth rises to my cheeks. Anger. I calm myself, using the techniques I learned in therapy. Anger doesn't have to be completely negative. We can learn from it, as long as it isn't misplaced.

This isn't misplaced. I don't want Travis humping this innocent young woman. And she *is* innocent. I can tell by her demeanor.

She's frightened of something.

I nod and smile at Travis. "Guess I screwed up. See you, man."

I whisk away to one of my other tables and take an order, glancing back at Zee Wolfe and Katelyn. Johnny just brought their tap water, and Katelyn takes a drink and then pats her lips with her pale yellow napkin.

And I want to be that napkin.

Breathe in. Breathe out.

No dates. No women. Not until I'm sure I can handle it.

I can still look, though.

And my God, she is beautiful.

3

KATELYN

"Penny for your thoughts," Zee says.

I meet her gaze. I'm always amazed at how beautiful and put-together she is. After all, I know her history, and though it's slightly better than mine, she should still be a mess.

"I'm not thinking about anything," I tell her.

It's a lie. I'm thinking about how handsome our waiter is. He has dark brown hair—nearly black—and even darker eyes. There's something about them. They look almost... unnatural, but in a completely beautiful way. Black and red swirls of a tattoo crawl up his left hand and then disappear beneath the long sleeve of his white button-down. It's impossible to tell what the complete picture is, and I find myself—surprisingly—itching to know.

"It's okay," she says. "He's attractive."

I pop my eyes open. "Are you a mind reader now?"

She smiles. "You blushed when he talked to you."

True. My cheeks warmed, and frankly, they're still warm.

"I know it seems strange to find a man attractive. Believe me, I felt the same way when I began to fall for Reid. When you've been though something so horrific, you wonder if you'll ever feel normal again. But you will. And this is your first clue."

"Because I think our waiter is hot?"

"Sure. It proves you're still yourself. I assume you were attracted to men before...everything."

"Yeah."

"And now you're still attracted to men."

"That doesn't mean I want to be with anyone."

"Of course it doesn't. But it should help you see that you *will* get through this. You did great at the center. You wouldn't be here if you didn't."

I nod. I know all this. Still, the force of my attraction to our server jolted me.

I didn't expect it to happen so quickly.

"Were you attracted to any of the men at the center?" Zee asks.

"There weren't very many men at the center. And the ones who were... I guess I found some of them attractive, but I wasn't thinking in those terms then."

"Very normal. And now that you're back in the real world, you're beginning to think in those terms again."

"Zee, our server is really good-looking. Any woman—and probably a lot of men—would find him handsome."

"True." Zee glances at the menu that's open before her. "But it's a step in the right direction that *you* do."

Zee is studying psychology. She told me all about her original ambition—to go to college and medical school and become a physician. But after...everything, she decided to study psychology instead, to help others like herself. She still hasn't ruled out med school, but she needs an undergraduate degree first, and for that, she's studying psychology.

She finished one semester, but now she's on maternity leave.

"I never asked," I say. "Do you know the sex of your baby?"

"It's a girl," she says softly. "A little girl. She's going to be spoiled rotten by her daddy."

"Have you decided on a name?"

"No. Reid and I can't seem to agree. Obviously, neither of us were close to our parents, and Reid loves his sister, but he doesn't want to hijack her name. I wish there were someone we could honor."

"How about that, then?"

"What?"

"Honor?"

"You mean as a name?"

"It's a beautiful name. Honor Wolfe."

A smile splits Zee's pretty face. "I love it. I absolutely love it! I have to text Reid. I hope he loves it as much as I do."

"What names were you considering?" I ask.

"Nothing we can agree on, like I said. He likes Isabella, and I like Morgan. Two totally different names. But Honor... I think we both may be able to get behind that one." She taps a message into her phone.

"Are you ready to hear about the specials, ladies?"

I jerk toward Luke's deep voice. And when I say deep, I mean really deep. Like James Earl Jones deep, only with a sexy rasp.

His dark hair is slightly wavy, and it's cut short. Not

normally my cup of tea, but he makes it sexy. I stare at his left hand again, but I still can't tell what those black and red swirls lead to.

His eyes are so dark. Nearly black like the onyx-colored sea glass that washed up on the beach while I was on the island. I suppose not all of Treasure Island was bad. The color of Luke's eyes exists in nature on that island. Not so unnatural after all. Perhaps what's unnatural—and beautiful —is the way he's looking at me. He seems kind. Not like the men on the island who used to look at me.

"Sure, Luke," Zee says. "Please tell us about the specials."

"We have a trimmed ribeye with horseradish hollandaise. Comes with a loaded baked potato and braised broccolini. And we have a broiled mahi mahi with port wine reduction and a really amazing mushroom risotto. I tried it myself. It's delicious."

"Any of that sound good to you, Katelyn?" Zee asks.

"I don't eat red meat," I say.

"You'll love the mahi mahi, then." Luke smiles.

God, he's even better-looking when he smiles.

I nod. "I'm not really into seafood. The chicken piccata looks good, though."

"You have my personal guarantee that you'll love it," he says, still smiling, and still making my heart beat faster than I want it to. "Mrs. Wolfe?"

"I'm not a big red meat eater, either," Zee says. "I'll try the mahi mahi special."

"Good enough. Anything else I can get you? A glass of wine?"

"Not for me, obviously." Zee pats her belly again.

"Me neither," I say almost automatically.

I haven't had a drink in... Well, not since I was rescued. I drank a lot on the island. Usually because whoever had me for the evening wanted me to.

I was actually one of the luckier ones. I was only hunted about half the time. Sometimes I was just booked for the night. I suppose it was better than running for my life. Garnet —I mean Aspen; I have to remember our real names—was hunted regularly. She's tall and muscular—a professional volleyball player at one time—and the men loved taking her down.

Gah! I don't want to think about this.

"No, thank you," I say.

Luke raises his eyebrows. "No thank you what?"

"I don't want any wine."

"Right. You already said that."

"Did I?"

Zee smiles at me and nods. "It's okay. Everything will be okay."

"I'll get the fish started for you." Luke whisks away from our table and stops at another.

I can't stop looking at him.

"He seems like a nice man," Zee says.

I force my gaze back where it belongs. On my dinner companion. My savior. We all owe the Wolfe siblings so much.

If not for them, the others and I would still be captive on that island.

"I'm sure he is," I say noncommittally.

"It's okay," she says. "It's okay to feel something."

"I don't feel anything. Except I find him attractive."

"I understand."

She lets it drop, thank goodness.

I don't want to think about this anymore.

Because if I do, I'll have to acknowledge that she's right.

I *do* feel something. It's not anything I'm familiar with, but it's a positive emotion.

And that scares the hell out of me.

4

LUKE

I head to the kitchen to pick up an order—

"Oh!"

The voice comes from Katelyn's table.

I turn around and stride back quickly.

But it's not Katelyn.

It's Mrs. Wolfe.

Katelyn is next to her.

"What happened?" I ask. "Is she all right?"

"I... I think my water broke," Zee says.

"Oh..." For someone who's seen nearly everything, I freeze. I have no idea what to do.

Katelyn rises. "I have to call her husband."

"I can do it." Zee grabs her phone off the table. "My due date isn't for two weeks yet."

"I don't think little Honor cares about your due date," Katelyn says. "What can I do?"

"I'm literally sitting in a puddle," Zee says. "I'm not sure there's anything anyone *can* do."

Finally, my mind comes back to life and I whip my phone out of my pocket. "I'm calling 911."

"Please, don't go to all that trouble. Reid will get here and he'll take me to the hospital. Everything's all set."

"Are you sure?"

Zee taps into her phone. "Yes, I'm sure. Oh!"

Katelyn gasps. "Are you okay?"

"Yes, fine. Just a little gas or something."

"It's probably a contraction," Katelyn says.

"No, it can't be. Just because my water broke doesn't mean I'm going to have contractions right away. We learned about all of this in Lamaze class."

I ignore Zee's advice and call 911 just as my manager, Lois, reaches the table. "Mrs. Wolfe! Are you all right?"

"She's in labor," Katelyn says.

"I'll get an ambulance right away."

"I'm on it," I tell Lois with my phone to my ear.

"Thank you for calling 911," the dispatcher says into my ear, "what is your emergency?"

"We need an ambulance at The Glass House in Manhattan. One of our diners is in labor. Her water just broke. It's Zee Wolfe. Reid Wolfe's wife."

"I'll get it dispatched. Thank you."

"They're sending an ambulance," I tell Lois.

"Good. Thanks, Luke. Mrs. Wolfe, let me help you up. You can lie down in our staff lounge while you wait for the ambulance."

"Goodness, I'm sorry about the chair," Zee says.

"Don't worry about that. Please. May I help you up?"

"No, no. I'm truly fine." Zee stands, and of course the back of her navy blue skirt is wet.

This isn't the first time I've seen a woman's water break, although the last time was a long time ago.

A time better left forgotten, especially now.

I take her arm. "Let me help you."

"That's kind of you. Thank you, Luke."

I lead her toward the restrooms to a door designated "staff only." The Glass House is a top notch restaurant, and it doesn't skip on the lounge for the staff. A long comfortable couch sits along the back wall.

Katelyn walks toward it, grabs two pillows from a loveseat, and places them on one side of the couch. "These will help you get comfortable."

"You guys are making way too much of a fuss," Zee says. "I'm fine, and Reid's on his way."

"He'll hit traffic," I say. "The ambulance will get here first."

Zee chuckles. "You don't know Reid Wolfe."

She's right. I don't. But I know a lot of people *like* Reid Wolfe. They may *think* they control everything, but no one controls Manhattan traffic.

"Can I get you anything?" Lois asks. "Water?"

"No, thank you," Zee says. "Unless you have a change of clothes for me."

"We may have something."

"Goodness, I was kidding. I hate that I'm ruining everything I sit on."

"It's just amniotic fluid," Katelyn says.

Which is mostly urine. I don't enlighten them with this fact, though. Not the time. They'd just wonder how I know.

"I need to get back to my tables," I say. "Let me know if you need anything, Lois."

Lois nods with a weak smile. "I will. Thank you, Luke. You've been a big help.

I'm not sure I've done much, but I walk backward, toward the door, unable to take my eyes off Katelyn. I don't want to leave her, and I sure as hell don't want to have this feeling.

Feelings like this were what got me into trouble, and I can't relive that.

Finally I make it to the door and take a quick trip to the restroom to wash my hands, just in case I got any pee—er....amniotic fluid—on them.

Then back to work.

Two of my orders are up, and Travis is taking care of them for me. I owe him one. I check in with all my customers, fill a few water glasses for the busboy, and then look back toward the door to the staff lounge.

Should I warn anyone that an ambulance is on its way? That any minute now, paramedics are going to rush in wielding a stretcher for Reid Wolfe's wife?

The soft music drifting through the room stops.

"Ladies and gentlemen," comes Lois's voice. "I'm sorry to disturb your dinner, but I want to let you know that one of our diners has gone into labor. An ambulance will be arriving soon, and we'll do our best not to disrupt your meals. You'll all be receiving ten percent off your dinner checks tonight."

Collective *oohs* and *ahs* drift through the restaurant.

Lois is a good manager. She just made all her customers happy with a mere mention of a small discount.

She also just cost me ten percent of my tips. Most customers forget that they're supposed to tip on the full price of the meal.

Oh, well.

Not like I need the money, but Travis and the others will feel it.

Not my problem.

Funny, I don't say that nearly as much as I used to. Now I feel like it *is* my problem. These people are my friends. I should've given the table to Travis when he asked for it. Normally, I would have. I don't care about tips.

But I didn't want to lose out on meeting Katelyn.

And now?

Katelyn's leaving, and neither Travis nor I will get the tip from the table.

Fuck it all.

5

KATELYN

"Can I do anything?" I ask Zee.

"No. I'm sorry about this. I'll call a cab to take you home."

"I can take care of that myself. You just concentrate on labor."

"It's not labor. Not yet anyway. I haven't had a contraction since that one at the table and that was...how long ago?"

I check my phone. "Ten minutes? Maybe fifteen? I wasn't really paying attention."

"Here." She hands me her phone. "See what time I texted Reid.

I take a look. "Zee?"

"Yeah?"

"You wrote out the text, but you didn't hit send."

She gasps. "What?"

"See?" I show her. "So I have no idea what time it was, and Reid doesn't know you're in labor."

"Damn! Pregnancy brain. It's a thing. Can you send it, please?

"Of course." I hit send. "We still don't know how long ago you had that first contraction."

"Find Luke. See what time he called 911. That'll give us our best clue."

"O...kay. But I'm not sure I should leave you."

"I'm fine. The paramedics are on the way, and I'm going to have to be able to tell them how far apart the contractions are. Right now, I can't do that."

"Got it. I'll find him."

I leave the lounge, glancing back at Zee. She seems comfortable enough. Still, I don't feel right leaving her.

Or am I just fearing talking to a man I find attractive?

I stopped looking at men that way long ago. Sure, some of the men who came to Treasure Island were attractive—but they also came to hunt women. To fuck women. To treat women like disposable objects.

So their physical attractiveness became repugnant. They were all repugnant, no matter what they looked like.

Then there was...

I lean against the wall between the door to the staff lounge and door to the men's restroom.

And images flash before me.

∾

It's my first night on display.

That's what they call it. I fought as hard as I could, but I'm still here. On display.

The pain in my shoulders has finally subsided, all my bruises have faded.

And now I'm on display.

A woman called Diamond explained everything. Men will

come. Men will come and look me over, as if I'm a side of beef hanging in the butcher shop. If one of them likes what he sees, he can take me for the evening. Do what he wants with me. Anything. Except he can't kill me.

I have to force myself to become numb to the concept.

"They won't put you out in the hunting grounds right away," Diamond said this morning. "They start you out slowly, so you get used to what will happen."

"How does anyone get used to this?" I demanded. "We're people, Diamond. People, not animals. I wouldn't treat an animal this way."

"You wouldn't," she said, "but there are those who do. Not all animals are hunted for food. Some for sport."

"It's wrong," I said, "and it's doubly wrong to do it to people."

She didn't respond, but her eyes did.

She agreed. She didn't like what went on here.

Why didn't she do something to stop it?

I sit here now, wearing nothing but a tropical print halter top and a sarong around my waist. Onyx sits next to me. I don't know her actual name. We're forbidden to use our old names here.

"It'll be okay," she says to me through trembling lips.

It's Onyx's first evening too.

I fear for her. I want to fight for her, but then I selfishly hope she gets chosen and I don't.

She's beautiful. Much more beautiful than I am, with her long dark hair and gorgeous nearly black eyes.

I'm not beautiful enough to be here.

So why was I brought here?

Every woman here, including Diamond herself, is supermodel stock.

And I—

The door opens, and—I count quickly—ten gentlemen—not

gentlemen, actually—stride in. Their lascivious gazes rake over us, fifteen total, and some women I've never seen until tonight.

We're told not to make eye contact with the men. No problem there. I don't want to look at any of them, and I certainly don't want to...

Nausea spikes in my throat. How can I do this?

But Diamond warned us. If we can't do it on our own, we'll be given drugs.

I don't want drugs.

So I'll do this.

What other choice do I have?

A large hand closes over mine.

I don't look up. It doesn't matter who he is or what he looks like. I don't look at him unless I'm told to.

"What's your name?" His voice isn't overly low but it is commanding.

I still don't look up. "Moonstone," I say softly, my voice cracking slightly.

He clears his throat. "I'll take you. Come with me."

6

LUKE

She stands next to the men's room, her eyes closed, her palms flattened against the wall, as if she needs its support to keep from crumpling to the floor.

"Katelyn?"

She flinches but doesn't open her eyes.

I want to reach out to her, to touch her, but if I do, she may flinch even more, and I don't want that. I don't want to do anything to harm this woman—or any woman. Not ever again.

"Katelyn?" I say again.

One eye opens this time and then the other.

"Is Mrs. Wolfe okay?"

The blare of the sirens in the distance drifts through to us. They're coming closer.

I turn toward the sound. "It won't be long now. We should go tell Mrs. Wolfe."

Katelyn doesn't respond, nor does she move.

"I'll do it."

I turn toward the door to the staff lounge when Lois

comes rushing toward us. "They're almost here. We'll need to stay out of their way."

"Yeah, of course." I turn back to Katelyn. "We need to move. The paramedics are coming."

She nods then, and when I tentatively take her hand, she doesn't resist. I'm not sure where I'm going to take her. The staff lounge is off limits. The paramedics will head straight for that room. Back to her table? No. She needs quiet. Peace.

I don't know how I know this, but I do.

Her hand is freezing cold, but still a spark shoots through me at the contact.

Outside?

Not really an option either. The paramedics will be blocking everything and we'll have to walk somewhere to get away from them. I don't want Katelyn to have to walk any more than necessary until she comes out of this funk.

Through the kitchen, then. The paramedics won't go there, and there's a doorway to the back alley, where we get deliveries.

"Come on."

To my surprise, she doesn't resist. She follows behind me, her hand still in mine, as we stride through the kitchen.

"Everything okay?" the pastry chef asks me.

"Yeah, Trina. This young woman just needs some air, and the ambulance is arriving for Mrs. Wolfe."

Trina nods, and no one else questions me as we walk through the clattering sounds of the kitchen and through the door to the delivery entrance.

A stray yellow cat whisks by, and Katelyn gasps.

"It's just a cat, honey. Just a cat. What can I do for you?"

"I should be with Zee."

"The paramedics will take care of her."

"But...she took such good care of me. I need to be there for her."

"All right. I'll take you back in if that's what you want."

She nods, so back through the door we go, through the kitchen, and out into the—

"Where the hell is my wife?"

The loud bellow comes from an Armani-clad businessman with black hair and wide blue eyes. Reid Wolfe. He looks just like his photos. I've never met him, but for a hot second, we traveled in the same circles. We're the same age. Thirty-three.

Lois rushes to him. "Mrs. Wolfe is fine, Mr. Wolfe. She's resting in the staff lounge. Come with me. The paramedics are on their way."

Reid Wolfe looks stunned. His normally perfectly coiffed head of hair is sticking up in strange places, and his tie is loose and his jacket wrinkled. He and Lois disappear into the lounge.

The sirens get louder, and within another thirty seconds, paramedics are rushing in with a stretcher.

Katelyn gasps and freezes.

What now?

"Come on." I take her back through the kitchen and outside into the alley again.

No cat this time. The sirens probably scared all the strays away. Sometimes, during my break, instead of going to the lounge, I come out here and bring scraps to the strays. There's a mongrel I like. He has a blue merle coat and one blue eye and one brown eye. I named him Jed.

He's not here tonight, but he'll be back, looking for his evening meal. Once the commotion dies down.

"Easy," I say to Katelyn. "She's fine. Her husband's here, and the ambulance will take her to the hospital."

"I should have been stronger," Katelyn says.

"Stronger?"

"I should have stayed with her. I owe her everything."

"It's okay. She'll understand." I have no idea if this is true, but what else can I say? What exactly does Katelyn owe Mrs. Reid Wolfe?

"She... She brought me here."

"Don't worry. I'll get you a cab. Everything will be fine."

She meets my gaze then. Truly meets my gaze, and I realize it's the first time she's done so.

Her eyes are beautiful, a light blue like the summer sky. The lightest blue I've ever seen, actually. And her hair, it's also lighter than I thought. It's not a honey blond but more of an ash blond. Not a dark root in sight. This is her natural color.

Her face is a perfect oval shape with high cheekbones and a rosy blush. Her lips full and pink, and parted just so...

I can't help myself.

I lean toward her and brush my lips over hers.

She gasps and jerks backward, her back hitting the brick wall of the building. Her blue eyes widen nearly into circles, and her pupils dilate.

She's scared.

Scared of me.

I don't want her to be scared of me. I'm done scaring women. That was the old me. The new me...

Well, I don't really know him yet, but I do know that he doesn't want to scare women.

Especially not *this* woman.

I'm sorry. The words don't make it to my lips. Because

they're only partially true. I don't lie anymore—at least not beyond what's necessary for my survival. That's no longer me. So to say a blanket "I'm sorry" would be a lie. I'm truly sorry if I scared her, but I'm adamantly *not* sorry I kissed her.

I'd do it again.

And again.

In fact, all my strength is required at this very moment not to push her into the brick wall, shove my tongue into her mouth, and grind my quickly hardening dick into her belly.

But I made a promise to myself. No relationships—other than a few friendships—until I'm sure I'm ready. Until I'm sure I'm fully healed.

I will abide my promise. If I can't keep a promise to myself, how will I ever keep a promise to Katelyn or anyone else?

I move backward a few steps, creating much-needed distance between us.

Then the words. "I didn't mean to frighten you."

And then her words...

"You didn't."

L uke's eyebrows shoot up.

I can't blame his surprise. My words surprised me as well. Indeed, I certainly *acted* frightened—gasping and backing away from him.

In truth, though?

The kiss felt...*right*, somehow.

The soft press of his lips to mine. Like butterfly wings. He didn't push. He didn't prod. He didn't attempt to force my mouth open. He didn't grab my breast.

Pure gentleness. That's what it was.

Something I've never experienced before.

Even now, my heart beats like a hummingbird's. And it's not from fear.

I know fear better than most people do, and this isn't it.

This is something I've never experienced. It's a little scary for sure, but good scary. Good meaning I want to feel it again. I want to see where it goes.

Luke takes a step toward me. "I didn't?"

"No, you didn't."

He reaches toward me, hesitating. Then he touches the apple of my cheek lightly. So lightly I almost don't feel it. Except I *do* feel it. I feel it all the way down to my toes.

I force myself not to shy away from his touch. Yes, I must force myself, even though something inside me desperately wants his touch.

A touch from a man I don't even know. Who I only just met.

So odd.

For someone who spent the last ten years being touched by men she didn't know, I have no idea why I want that now.

I want him to kiss my lips again. And I *don't* want it just as much, because I know I'm not ready for it.

I'm nowhere close to healed from the trauma I endured, but I've healed enough to be on my own, to take back my life.

And I wonder...

What if taking back my life means taking back my body as well? Deciding for myself who to let touch me? Kiss me?

Of course it does. I've had enough therapy to know the answer, but I never really thought about what it truly meant until now. This moment.

Luke takes another tentative step forward. Only about a foot separates us now, and his hand still softly caresses my cheek.

"May I..."

My heart still pounds. So quickly I wonder if this is even healthy. But I already know my answer.

I nod. "Yes. Please."

Another brush of his lips. And he has the most beautiful full lips I've ever seen on a man.

Another peck, and then another. Then he lets his lips slide over mine, and I...

God, should I?

I part my lips slightly.

He doesn't rush in, even though I almost want him to. Instead, he softly slides his tongue over my lower lip and then probes between them.

I stifle a gasp when our tongues meet.

It's still a soft kiss. He's letting me lead him.

Part of me wants him to dive right in, take control. But that part of me isn't my brain, and I need to keep my brain focused at the moment.

I don't know this man. He could be anyone.

But his gentleness...

He's kind. In my heart, I know this.

If I want a deeper kiss, I'm going to have to give him a signal, and though my body is telling me to go for it, I don't.

Not yet.

Not with a man I just met.

I've had enough of doing things with a man I just met.

This time, I want to go slowly. Get to know my partner. And if Luke isn't interested in going that route? I'll walk away.

I'll be strong, and I'll walk away.

I have to. For myself. To take it all back. Not just my body, but my life. My *self*.

No matter how much he makes my heart sing.

And it's singing. It's singing in a way I never could have imagined.

I was a mere eighteen when I was taken. I'm pushing close to thirty now, and I'm both experienced and inexperienced. I need to go slowly.

Oh, this kiss.

So easily I could part my lips just a little more, wrap my arms around his neck and pull him even closer.

So easily...

But I don't. I twist my head, and his lips slide to my cheek. A breeze hits me, cooling my skin where his lips have trailed a path of wetness.

Luke steps back. "Are you okay?"

All I can do is nod. I don't trust myself to try to speak. The thoughts whirling in my head are...jumbled. Just thoughts and feelings and single words.

I'm not sure what would come out if I tried to talk.

"You want me to get you a cab?"

"Yeah. Thanks."

"Come on." He takes my hand. "If I stay out here any longer I'll be out of a job."

"Oh!" I clamp my hand to my mouth. "I'm so sorry. I'm keeping you from your work. Forgive me. I wasn't thinking."

He smiles. "There's nothing to forgive. I'm out here with you because I want to be. Lois is cool. She'll probably understand. If not?" He shrugs. "I'll get another job easy. I'm a crazy good server."

A chuckle escapes my throat. An actual chuckle. Not quite a laugh, but I'll take it.

Boy, it's been a long time. A *really* long time.

I guess I laughed a few times at the center. I think I did. A couple of the residents were really funny. The kind who hide their hurt under an armor of jokes. I felt for them, but they were pretty darned funny. And even though I know they were covering up their own pain, I'll always remember them—and be grateful to them—for making me smile. Sometimes even laugh.

But this. Luke. This chuckle is more of a laugh than I've had since...well...since, before.

"Did I say something amusing?" he asks, his eyes sparkling.

"You did. And thank you."

"Thank me? What? You don't think I'm a crazy good server?"

"Luke, I know you are, even though I have no knowledge other than you taking our orders. Thank you. For making me laugh. For... For everything."

"My pleasure"—he touches my cheek once more —"Katelyn."

A spark. A real honest-to-goodness spark. It shoots right through Luke's fingertips and into my cheek, and then it darts downward.

All the way downward.

To that place. That place that knows nothing but force and pain. Violation and greed.

I feel the spark there.

And...

I'm a little less afraid of the future.

8

LUKE

"Where do you live?" I ask Katelyn once we're back inside the restaurant.

She rattles off the address in a monotone, and I commit it to memory. I pull out my phone to call her a cab when I realize I don't need to. This is New York, not LA. Cabs are a dime a dozen here. All we have to do is walk out the front door and we'll find one.

I guide Katelyn through the restaurant, when—

"Luke!" Lois scurries toward me. "You need to relieve Travis. He's been handling your tables *and* his."

"Right. I'm sorry, Lois. I was taking care of Mrs. Wolfe's friend."

Lois's demeanor changes at the mention of Mrs. Wolfe. "Of course! Are you all right?" she asks Katelyn.

"Yes, I'm fine. Luke has been a big help. I'm just so worried about Zee."

"The paramedics said everything looked under control. I'm sure she and Mr. Wolfe will have some good news soon."

"Katelyn," I say, "take care of yourself."

"I will. Thank you again, Luke."

"You know," Lois says, "your shift is over in an hour anyway. Why don't you go ahead and take the rest of the evening off, Luke? As a personal thank you from me for being such a help with Mrs. Wolfe and her friend."

I try not to let my eyes pop out of their sockets. Lois is a good and fair manager, but this still surprises me. "Are you sure?"

"Yes. I'd feel much better if you waited with Ms...." She lifts her eyebrows at Katelyn.

"Brooks," Katelyn says. "Katelyn Brooks."

Brooks. Now I have a last name and an address. I file the information away.

"Okay. Thanks, Lois. I'll see you tomorrow, then."

"You're off tomorrow."

"Right. See you the day after, then."

"Don't be late." Lois smiles and then heads back to the front of the restaurant.

I follow, leading Katelyn through the crowd of people waiting for a table and out the door.

Several yellow cabs are already waiting outside the restaurant. "Here, you go. It was really nice meeting you, Katelyn."

She smiles. "You too, Luke." She doesn't let go of my hand.

"You know," I say, thinking out loud, "you don't live far from here. Only three blocks. Instead of a cab, what if I walked you home?"

Her eyes widen. "In the dark?"

"It's dark, yes. I wouldn't want you walking alone. But I promise you're safe with me. Besides, this is downtown Manhattan. It's well lit."

For the first time, I wonder what Katelyn does for a living.

She lives in an expensive neighborhood. Expensive even for Manhattan. Near the Wolfe building. She either comes from money or works with the Wolfes. Why else would she be having dinner with Zee Wolfe?

"It's really safe?"

Her question confounds me. It's dark, but it's not late. And she has a male escort. I scan the area. Male-female couples are everywhere, walking, laughing, talking. Groups of women walk together as well.

Why is she so reticent?

"I promise to get you safely home," I say, "but if you're more comfortable in a cab—"

"No." She stops me. "I think I'd like to walk with you."

I can't help myself. A giant smile splits my face. I don't know why, but I'm relishing this extra fifteen minutes I'm going to have with Katelyn.

And it's not because I loved kissing her, which I did.

It's not because she's beautiful, which she is.

It's not because I've changed, which I have.

It's because, deep inside, I know I'm feeling something I've never felt before.

And it feels good. Damned good.

"Tell me something about yourself," I say.

She doesn't reply at first, and just when I think she isn't going to, she finally says, "I'm...looking for a job."

Interesting. She doesn't work for the Wolfes after all. "Oh? What kind of job?"

"Anything, really. I'm not really qualified for much."

"Do you have a degree?"

"College? No. But I did finish high school."

"What other jobs have you had recently?"

"I just moved here."

41

"Where did you live before?"

Again, she stays silent for a few seconds, and I wonder if she won't answer.

Finally, "I'm from LA originally."

"Really? So am I."

Shit. I'm not supposed to say that. I've got to be more careful.

"Are you?"

"Well, not LA exactly." Maybe I can fix this. "Northern California."

"Why'd you say LA, then?"

"I didn't. You did." No lie there. All I said was *so am I.*

She doesn't push me, and I'm grateful.

"So what kind of work did you do in LA?" I prompt.

"I was... I was in the escort business."

I stop my jaw from dropping. "You don't mean..."

"No. Just a paid escort. You know, to social events." She watches her feet as we walk. "But I don't want to do that anymore. Unfortunately, it doesn't leave me qualified for much else than to look pretty on someone's arm."

And I bet she was the belle of the ball wherever she went.

I'm no stranger to beautiful LA women, and Katelyn is in a class by herself. Now that she mentioned LA, I can totally see it. Light blond hair and blue eyes, beach body, perfectly creamy skin that looks good with any color of gown. Did she attend the Oscars on a celebrity's arm? The Emmys? Grammys? Hollywood premieres?

I don't doubt it, and a sliver of jealousy spikes into me. Odd. Not because I'm jealous. That's normal. It's even normal to want to pummel all the rich men who probably escorted her to galas and benefits. What's odd is that I no longer have the urge to lock her away to keep her safe and under my control. Sure, I want to protect her, but within reason.

I've come a long way.

And that makes me smile.

"Do you want me to ask Lois if there's a place for you at the restaurant?"

"I've never waited tables. And I'm horrible in a kitchen."

"What about hosting?"

"I've never done that."

"Hmm...I don't know if you're qualified. It requires a lot of wearing sharp clothes and looking pretty."

"I'm sure there's more to it than that."

"Of course. Can you read?"

"I think I just told you I'm a high school graduate."

"That doesn't always mean much, but I was only kidding. I know you can read, Katelyn. That's all hosting requires. You read the reservations list, or you take names. You answer the phone to take reservations, and you lead people to their table. I'm pretty sure none of that is beyond your capabilities."

"As I recall, The Glass House already has a lovely hostess and a maître d'."

"Sure. We have several. Doesn't mean there isn't room for another."

She pauses a moment. "I'm not sure I'm good enough with people."

"You were an escort, Katelyn. You must be good with people."

Silence again. "Maybe. I can type, you know. I think I'd rather type."

"And be stuck in a cubicle all day? Working at a restaurant would be a lot more fun. Plus, important people come in all the time. You probably already know this, but you're gorgeous, Katelyn. Model gorgeous. Agents come in all the time looking for fresh faces."

"I'm way too old to be a model."

She may be right. I don't have a clue about modeling. All I know is she's the most spectacular-looking woman I've seen in a long time, including my time in LA, where spectacular-looking women threw themselves at me on a regular basis.

"I'm not looking to get discovered or anything," she says. "I left LA to get away from all that."

"And you came to Manhattan."

More silence. She must know that her reasoning makes no sense at all.

Then again, I shouldn't be in Manhattan either. I should be on a farm in a flyover state, but I couldn't leave the city life totally behind, even though I hate New York.

"I have...friends here," she finally says.

"The Wolfes?"

"Zee Wolfe, yes. She's my friend."

"How did you two meet?"

Silence again.

And this time she never replies.

9

KATELYN

Does he notice I don't answer? It doesn't matter, anyway, as we arrive at my building.

Luke's eyes widen. "You live here?"

I nod.

"And you're not working?"

"No, not at the moment."

"How do you—"

"The Wolfes. Zee. She's...loaning me some money until I get settled here." I don't like the lie, but I'm not ready to talk about why I'm really here. Luke will run away screaming.

"Good for you, then," he says. "What floor are you on?"

"Ten."

"I'll walk you up."

"No, that's okay."

Men aren't allowed in this building. Okay, that's not quite true. Fathers and brothers are allowed. Good friends. But we're not supposed to bring dates here...because we're not supposed to be dating.

"Katelyn, I don't mind."

"This building is very safe. Great security."

At least that part isn't a lie. I pull the keycard out of my purse. One card to get in the building. One for the elevator. One for my actual apartment. Plus a guard on duty inside at all times.

Is that normal? In Manhattan? I have no idea. Will it seem strange to Luke? I should ask Zee.

Except Zee is busy giving birth. She won't be around to take my calls any time of the day anymore. She'll be resting and caring for a newborn.

I exhale a long breath. I didn't realize how much I've come to depend on her in just a few days.

She visited the retreat center on the island several times a month, but not the last two months because she couldn't fly so late in her pregnancy. Still, she was only a phone call or text away.

I was one of the first women to leave the center. I still have a lot of healing to do, but I couldn't be "kept" any longer. We were always free to leave the center. It was certainly more freedom than any of us had while we were prisoners. Still...I felt caged.

Caged and taken care of.

I want to be free.

I'm still not. I'm living in housing—really nice housing—provided by the Wolfes. I have no choice. But I'll find work as soon as I can.

Remember your strength, Katelyn. You're safe here. You don't need Zee to hold your hand.

"Katelyn..."

I inhale. "Please. Please, Luke. Don't fight me on this."

He nods then, though his eyes look...shadowed and sad. "I'd like to see you again."

"Well"—I clear my throat—"you know where I live."

That wasn't the best thing to say. I basically just invited him to come back here, which is a really bad idea. I hardly know him. He shouldn't even be here.

Sure, I know what his lips feel like on mine. I *like* how his lips feel on mine.

But I don't *know* him.

I'm far from ready to go on a date or anything. I'm not supposed to be dating. Not that I'm bound not to, but my therapist suggested waiting a while longer, and frankly, I agree with her.

"I do. Could I have your number?"

Number. Yeah. He should call me. Not show up here. Much better. "Sure. Okay." I rattle off the digits.

He inputs them into his phone. "I'm off tomorrow. Would you like to do something?"

"I'll be...looking for a job."

"Dinner, then?"

"I..."

"Katelyn, you gave me your number. I told you I want to see you again. If that's not what you want, tell me now, and I'll delete the number. No pressure."

Yes. Yes. I should tell him to do that. Delete the number. He's not my type. He has dark hair and tattoos. I'm used to...

God, I'm used to billionaires in tailored suits with no tattoos.

Just because a man looks clean cut doesn't mean he's a good person. I know that better than anyone.

Anyone.

I've seen men clad in designer clothing and Italian leather shoes change into fatigues and prey on women as if they were animals.

I swallow against the sour in my throat.

This. This is why it's too soon for me to even think about seeing a man.

Even this man, who doesn't look anything like the men who abused me, violated me.

Who also doesn't look like any of the surfer boys I knew before.

"Message received," Luke says, pulling his phone back out.

I touch his arm. Even through his long-sleeved white shirt, I feel muscles...and a massive spark.

He lifts his eyebrows.

"Don't," I say. "Don't delete my number."

A smile nudges at his lips. "You sure?"

Sure? I'm not sure of anything in my life. For a long time, I wasn't sure the sun would rise the next day. I learned to live one day at a time. One more day of survival.

I inhale again. Deeply.

Then, "I'm sure."

"Dinner tomorrow, then?" he asks, a tinge of hopefulness in his deep voice.

"Okay, but text me where, and I'll meet you."

"I don't mind picking you up, Katelyn."

I know, but *I* mind. "I'll be out and about searching for work. It'll be easier that way."

I'm pretty sure he doesn't buy my excuse, but he doesn't push.

"Got it," he says. "I'll text you. Or I'll call you."

"You don't have to call."

"I may want to hear your voice."

Another spark of warmth flows through me, landing in

that place once more. That place I wasn't sure would ever feel anything again. If it ever did.

"Your cheeks are red, Katelyn." Luke feathers his fingers over one.

Sparks again.

He leans in.

I back away.

He backs away.

Kiss me, please. Except don't. Except do.

"I'll see you tomorrow," he says.

He leans in again.

I back away.

"Goodnight," he says.

"Goodnight."

I slide my card through the slot and the door opens. I whisk inside and then stare through the glass in the door as Luke turns and walks back toward the restaurant.

I still feel his phantom lips on mine.

And I wish I hadn't backed away.

A lot of things don't jibe with Katelyn's story. The escort thing, for instance. I lived in LA. I know about those escort services. Sure, they say it's a no-sex transaction, but celebrities and businesspeople in LA have money. Lots of it. And it usually only takes a little to get the escort to bend the rules a little. Or a lot, depending on the woman.

I know.

I've been there. And I've paid.

Back in my other life, when I used to do things I'll never do again.

Escorts are outgoing, or they at least pretend to be. They're not going to get work if they don't turn on the charm.

While *I* find Katelyn charming, she's hardly outgoing. Some would pay just to have her beauty on their arm, but most want someone who'll be more than arm candy for the evening.

No way was Katelyn an escort.

Unless...

Unless something happened to her to make her crawl inside her shell.

There's no shortage of pigs in LA, either. I should know. I *was* one once. Until I turned my back on that life and became something even worse.

Which I choose not to think about at this moment.

Escorts are abused all the time. Sure, most of the time they consent to it in worship of the almighty dollar, but sometimes they don't.

And no one protects them, because the celebrity who did it pays everyone off.

It takes years for serial sexual abusers in LA to get what's coming to them, if they ever do at all. How many decades did that well known producer abuse women before he was brought down? Everyone knew.

Everyone.

I end up back at The Glass House to speak to Lois about a possible job for Katelyn. Lois is on duty until eleven, so she'll still be there.

Only a few customers are still dining, but the bar is full of patrons. Working with alcohol doesn't bother me as much as I thought it would. I got sober during my stay at the hospital. My mind functions a lot better now.

I hate who I used to be, and I try hard not to think about it. It creeps in sometimes, though. I have to deal with it. I can't outrun the past, no matter how hard I try, so I block it from my mind as much as I can..

I need to stay away from the past. For my own safety.

I shouldn't be getting involved with Katelyn or anyone else. I've been known to get involved too quickly. The old me, anyway.

The me who drank. The me who...did a lot of bad things.

Those things I try hard not to think about.

I'm far from ready to date a woman—especially a woman like Katelyn. She's beautiful, yes. But something is bothering her, haunting her.

Baggage.

I've got enough of my own to deal with. I sure don't need hers. Still, I'm going to take her to dinner tomorrow. And I'm going to ask Lois about a job for her.

I walk through the restaurant and find my manager in the back, talking to a couple at a two-top.

She looks up at me. "Luke? What are you doing back?"

"I want to talk to you for a minute."

"Sure. Let's go to the lounge." She excuses herself to the patrons.

I follow her to the staff lounge where Mrs. Reid Wolfe nearly gave birth. I steer clear of the couch.

She smiles. "I left a note for the day manager. He'll call to get it steam cleaned as soon as possible. In the meantime, I left a note on the bulletin board warning everyone what happened on the couch."

"It's just her water."

"Yeah, I know. But still..."

"Right. It's mostly urine."

She nods. "Yup. So what's up, Luke?"

"The woman who was with Mrs. Wolfe... Her name's Katelyn, and she's looking for work. I was wondering if you have any openings here at the restaurant."

"We can always use experienced servers," Lois says.

I inhale. "She'd be more of a host type."

"No serving experience?"

"Not that I know of."

"I don't need any hosts on my shift. I could check with the day managers."

Then she wouldn't be working with me. Our hours would clash. Which is maybe a good thing. This has to go slowly if it's going to go at all.

"Would you? She's a personal friend of Zee Wolfe's. I'm sure the Wolfe family would appreciate it."

"That's interesting."

"Is it?"

"Well...yeah. If she's that close to Mrs. Wolfe, why don't the Wolfes give her a job?"

Hmm. Good question, and I'm not sure why I didn't think of it. "Katelyn wants to do it on her own." Sure. That's probably the truth.

"Then shouldn't *she* be in here talking to me?"

"Yeah, and I'm sure she will be. She's doesn't know I'm asking."

This isn't going well.

"I'll email the day managers. See what's going on. Rachel and I are both fully staffed for evenings."

"Thanks, Lo. I appreciate it."

"Sure, no problem." She checks her watch. "I'm about ready to go. Trey's handling the kitchen cleanup tonight. Want to catch a drink somewhere?"

"I don't drink."

She cocks her head. "You don't? I guess I've never seen you drink, but I always see you on duty so you better not be drinking."

"I'm recovering, actually."

"Oh. No drink, then. Coffee?"

Is my manager asking me out? Or is this a friend thing? I'm not getting a good read on her. Lois is an attractive woman, but she pales next to Katelyn. Still, if I have coffee with her, maybe she'll go the extra mile to get Katelyn a job.

"I don't do caffeine in the evenings," I tell her, "but if you want a drink I can always put away a sparkling water with lime."

She smiles. "Sounds great. Let me grab my jacket. We can hit Zenobia's across the street."

Zenobia's is a bar with a small dance floor. It's a club for the people who can't get into one of the actual clubs. Tonight's a weeknight, so it won't be too crowded.

Lois and I take a seat at the bar. "A vodka tonic for me," she says to the bartender.

He nods toward me.

"Sparkling water with lime."

He raises his eyebrows slightly. Do I look like a drunk? I get the weirdest looks when I order a non-alcoholic beverage at a bar. A minute later, he slides the drinks in front of us. Lois gives him a credit card. "Run a tab."

A tab? How long does she think we're going to be here?

She takes a sip of her drink and lets out a sigh. "Mmm. Rough night at work, with Mrs. Wolfe going into labor and all. I've been gunning for a drink all night."

I bring my water to my lips and nod.

"So...recovering, huh?"

Everyone wants to know the story. I can't tell them the real one, of course, so I've got a canned speech ready.

"Yeah. I got into alcohol heavily when I was a teen because of my shitty home life. I've been sober for over ten years."

There's a grain of truth in there. The shitty home life part. I've only been sober for a few months, though, and I started drinking *way* before my teen years.

Most people don't ask too many questions after that.

Lois, apparently, isn't most people.

"Shitty home life? I'm sorry to hear about that. Is everything good now?"

"Good enough." I make my tone as noncommittal as I can. "Not something I talk about."

"Oh, sure. I get it." She takes another sip. "You want to dance?"

I down my water. "Sure. Why not?" I start to roll up the sleeves of my white button-down but then remember that I can't. The tattoo will attract more questions I can't answer. I'm still wearing my black dress pants that I work in.

I don't enjoy dancing all that much, but it's better than talking. I'm not sure what Lois's angle is, but when your boss asks you for a dance, you don't say no.

There's no band at this small venue, just a DJ spinning records. Or rather, toying with his Spotify account through a set of Bose speakers.

A few hip-hop songs, and I'm ready to call it a night, when a slow song begins.

Lois wraps her arms around my neck.

I guess we're still dancing.

She can't really be interested in me. Can she?

She leans into me. She's shorter than Katelyn and slightly curvier but not overweight at all. Attractive, with a brown bob and sparkling light brown eyes. Still...not my type.

If I even have a type anymore.

Yeah, I do.

Katelyn.

As I move slowly, another woman plastered against my body, only Katelyn fills my mind.

Already she's consuming me, and that's not great news.

I've been consumed by women before, and it never leads to anything good.

Of course, that was the old me.

The new me is...

Hell, I'm not even sure *who* the new me is. I don't know who I am anymore.

Which is another reason I shouldn't be starting anything. Especially with Katelyn, who, for reasons unknown, I already care about.

Recently moved, recently sober... Why not start a relationship? Man, what am I thinking?

The song comes to an end, thank God, and the DJ starts another fast number. Good timing for me to make a break for it. I pull away.

"Another drink?" I ask.

"Sure."

We head back to the bar, where Lois orders another round. I down mine quickly. "I should be going. Tomorrow's my day off and I have an early appointment."

"Oh?"

"Yeah. Dentist." I lie.

Lying isn't good. I used to lie a lot. I can't let myself fall into that habit again. Damn.

"Oh. Okay."

"You want me to get you a cab?" I ask.

"No. I think I'll stick around a little while longer. Thanks, though."

"Thanks for the drinks," I say. "Next time it's on me."

Her pretty brown eyes light up at the comment. Crap. I just intimated there'd be a next time, which there won't be.

Except she's my boss.

Double damn.

I could handle this. I could. Lois is a nice woman. I might even consider dating her if not for Katelyn. And if not for the fact that she's my boss. And if not for the fact that I shouldn't be dating anyone.

Easy enough. If she asks me out again, I'll give her the "you're my boss" line.

I may lose my job, but I can find another. Heck, I can even do a reverse #metoo move.

Except I won't. I can't. I need to stay under the radar. Filing lawsuits isn't the way to do that.

Under the fucking radar.

Dating a woman who could easily be a supermodel sure isn't the way to do that.

Working at a Manhattan restaurant isn't really the way to do that either.

I'm fucking this up. Majorly.

This being invisible thing isn't easy when you've been a celebrity your whole life.

11

KATELYN

H onor LaVonne Wolfe was born at five a.m. this morning.

I wake up to the text sent by Reid.

Reid Wolfe, COO of Wolfe Enterprises, billionaire, thought to send *me* a text when his daughter was born.

I'm amazed.

The younger Wolfes are nothing like their father. They're all wonderful.

I get up and shower quickly. I want to go to the hospital to see the baby, but it's not my place. Important people will be stopping by all day.

I'm hardly important.

Instead, I make myself an egg white omelet and then head to the first floor. There's a meeting today.

Meetings aren't required but highly recommended. I just moved in, so I have no idea what I'm in for. A support group most likely, though only two of us live here so far. Most of the women are still at the retreat center on the island.

I personally couldn't wait to get off that damned island.

I get it. The Wolfes took Treasure Island and made something good out of it. The center. An art colony. A resort.

But for me—and probably the other women who were held captive there—it will never be anything more than a prison.

A cage.

A place where unspeakable things were forced upon us.

I slide my card through the slot to call the elevator and head down to the first floor. Zee gave me a guided tour yesterday after all my clothing and other personals—which weren't much—arrived. I own basically nothing after being kept against my will for so long.

The first floor houses all the community areas. A gym, complete with a sauna and steam room. A lounge with vending machines and tables. A library, filled with everything from Aristotle to Nora Roberts. And a gathering room. Zee called it a fellowship hall, but that makes me think of church. I gave up believing in God ten years ago, so to me, it's a gathering room.

That's where I'm heading this morning.

Inside, the chairs are arranged in a circle. I feel like I'm walking into an AA meeting or something. Only one of the chairs is occupied.

An older woman with gray sprinkled through her dark hair looks up and meets my gaze. "Good morning."

I clear my throat. "Good morning."

"You must be Katelyn."

"I am, but how did you know?"

"Zee gave me a file with your photo in it." She rises and holds out her hand. A pearl bracelet circles her wrist. "I'm Dr. Macy Grimes, but please call me Macy. It's wonderful to have you here."

"Thank you."

Thank you? Why am I thanking her? Wonderful to have me here? When I'd rather not be here at all? When I'd rather that the circumstances leading me here never happened?

But they did happen.

No escaping that reality.

"So...what is this meeting about?"

"I'm here every morning."

"Every morning?" Surely I'm not supposed to come here every morning for group therapy.

"Yes. I'm here every morning, but we won't have meetings every morning. I'm here for all of you when you need someone to talk to."

"But the meeting..."

"Right. You asked what it's about. Twice a week we have group meetings. They're not required but recommended."

"Yes, I got the whole spiel." I don't mean to sound short. It just came out that way.

"You young ladies have been through a lot of therapy and healing already, but as you undoubtedly know, this is a lifetime process. A journey. We're all works in progress."

I'm thinking I'm a bigger work in progress than Macy is, but whatever.

"I see," I say.

"We're here to help each other." She eyes the door. "Lily is usually here right at nine. I hope she's okay."

Lily? I don't know any Lily. We used our actual names at the center, but who is Lily?

A woman rushes through the door then. She's light brown-skinned and beautiful. Her hair—which I remember as long—is now cut short in a cute bob.

"Lily," Macy says. "There you are. I was beginning to worry about you."

So this is Lily.

Except to me, her name is Tigereye. Of course we didn't go by our gem names at the center. Tigereye was called December.

I smile. "December?"

"Hi, Katelyn!" She rushes toward me and gives me a hug. "I changed my name to Lily. I hated the name December anyway. I don't know what my parents were thinking. I was born in March."

"Lily is beautiful. Is there a reason you chose it?"

"My favorite flower," she says. "Always lovely during any season."

I nod. I could have changed my name, but I chose not to. I was born Katelyn, and I'm still Katelyn. I was always Katelyn, even when I was Moonstone. Even when I couldn't remember my name.

I have to take it all back. Take my life back. And the first step seemed to be to take my name back.

"We're using last names now as well," Macy says. "So Katelyn Brooks, meet Lily Patel."

We hug again.

"Is Patel a new name too?" I ask her.

"No. It's my real last name. My father's from India. Is Brooks your old last name?"

I nod. "Just seems easiest," I say, though the name comes from my father, and there's no love lost between the two of us.

Still, he was happy to know I was alive and okay.

So was my mom.

They visited me at the center once, and they both wanted me to return to LA and live with them. But I figured Zee's offer was better for me. I can't get pulled back into my parents' drama when I'm still so fragile. My so called family is the reason I ended up on that island. Not my parents, but relatives—relatives they sent me to stay with.

Fragile. Yuck.

I hate the word.

But despite the strength I needed to endure the last ten years, I *am* fragile. Macy's right. It's a journey. I'll never be the Katelyn I was. I'm not sure I even want to be.

"We'll wait a few minutes to see if Aspen or Kelly show up," Macy says.

I raise my eyebrows. "Kelly? I thought only Aspen and Dec—sorry, Lily—were here."

"Kelly arrived late last night," Macy says.

"I don't think they'll show," Lily says.

Macy sighs. "You're probably right. Have you talked to Aspen?"

Lily nods. "She still doesn't feel comfortable talking to a group, and Kelly…"

Macy sighs again.

Kelly. I remember Kelly. Her gem name was Opal.

Kelly was…

Not friendly.

Most of us understood that we were in this together, but Kelly… She got jealous if someone else was chosen over her.

I used to pray someone else was chosen over me. Then of course I felt guilty about that, because I was praying for someone else to be hurt instead of me.

Then I stopped praying because clearly, God didn't exist.

No God could have let those horrors happen to me and to the others.

No God could let any of the horrors of the world happen.

And it was a man of God, a priest, who dislocated both my shoulders that time.

A fucking man of God.

Right.

God doesn't exist.

"Then it's just the three of us today." Macy smiles. "Please have a seat, both of you."

I take a seat a few chairs away from Macy. Sitting right next to her feels too...weird. Lily smiles and sits next to me.

"Today I want to talk about expectations," Macy begins. "This is a good topic for you especially, Katelyn, since you've just gotten here. It's important to keep our expectations normal."

Our expectations? I hate it when therapists do that. Act as if they've been through all the shit we've been through.

It's crap. Pure crap.

Macy goes on, "You've been through a lot of healing already, and I'm sure your therapists have told you that the road will have bumps. It will, and when you come to one, you have two choices. You can fall down or you can jump over it."

I resist the urge to roll my eyes. This is old news.

"Katelyn," she says to me, "do you have any expectations?"

"Not really," I reply.

"None at all?"

"No. This is my life now. I get that. I was dealt a shitty hand, but I'm alive. I'm glad to be alive. I guess I expect to stay alive. So yeah, I have an expectation. I sure didn't have that during the time on the island."

"That's good," Macy says.

Yup. Now she knows I'm not suicidal. One hurdle jumped.

"Anything else?" Macy asks.

"I'll find work. Make my own way. Take life one day at a time."

"Not a bad outlook at all. Lily?"

"I expect to be happy," she says. "And I will. Someday."

"That's a great expectation," Macy says, "and I have a piece of advice for both of you concerning happiness."

Again, I resist an eye roll. What can she possibly have to say to us about happiness after all we've been through?

"Think about this," Macy says, "because it's the truth. You don't have to wait until life is no longer difficult to be happy."

I meet Macy's gaze, as her words play in my mind.

It's the truth, she said.

I like the idea.

I like it a lot.

Life may always be difficult. Indeed, it probably will be. I've been dealt shitty cards.

Can I?

Can I be happy while I'm healing? While life is still hard?

Luke's image pops into my mind. Luke, with his dark hair and hypnotic eyes. His firm lips so soft against my own.

His red and black tattoo that probably goes all the way up his left arm.

I don't need a man to be happy. In fact, I'd probably be happier without a man, considering my past.

But I felt good with him. I felt *safe* with him.

Happy is a stretch. But good is a start.

I regard Macy. Sure, she's a Pollyanna with a doctorate who has probably led a sugar-and-spice life.

But her words...

You don't have to wait until life is no longer difficult to be happy.

And I know I'll be coming to meetings twice a week.

12

LUKE

The scar on my shoulder is a constant reminder of what I was.

What I no longer will allow myself to be.

I was fucked up. Majorly. I could blame my upbringing. My parents. My circumstances.

But in truth?

The only person to blame is myself. Once I became an adult, I made my own choices. Sure, there were extenuating circumstances that factored into those choices, but in the end, I made the decisions. I acted on them.

Power is an aphrodisiac. It crawls inside you. Clings to every microscopic cell in your body.

And it corrupts.

It corrupts from the inside out.

I look back now at the things I did, the people I hurt, and I don't want anything to do with power. If that means I spend the rest of my life waiting tables, so be it.

I can't lie. I miss the booze sometimes. Once an addict always an addict, as they say.

Yet I chose to work in a restaurant with a bar. To serve drinks to my customers. And every time I serve a martini—or a Manhattan, or a scotch and soda, or a glass of wine—the alcohol calls to me.

It's a constant battle—one I make a conscious choice to fight.

I can't let the demons lie, because if I do, they might return. I can't forget them for a moment.

Because I can't risk them taking me over once more.

My life was never difficult.

I was born to privilege. Too *much* privilege, really.

Now? Life is difficult. It's a constant challenge that I welcome. I finally see how the other half lives, and there's a certain beauty in it. A certain constancy.

And there's Katelyn.

Women are my other weakness. Booze and women. Man, they controlled my life. Sure, I *thought* I was in control. Even the women thought I was in control.

But that was always an illusion.

I hurt so many people, and I can never make it up to them. But I can at least live a clean and sober life. A clean and sober life without dragging Katelyn into it.

Even now, her beauty haunts me.

I must fight it. I can't be dragged back into my old habits.

I shouldn't have asked her to dinner tonight. I know it. On some level, I think she knows it as well.

My phone sits on my dresser, pulsing with an invisible heartbeat. So simple. I can just pull up her number, hit call, and tell her I changed my mind. That our dinner is off.

Yes, I should do that.

I pick up the phone. It's like a block of ice against my fingers.

I drop it, and it clatters onto the hardwood floor of my studio.

I leave it there and look around my sparse place.

I live in Manhattan. I shouldn't, but I do. I shouldn't work here, either. There's always a chance of running into people who may remember things I prefer them not to remember.

But living life anonymously in a small town... I couldn't do it. I tried. Okay, I didn't try that hard. But I did look into it.

You can take the boy out of the city, but you can't take the city out of the boy.

So I ultimately chose to stay in the city—New York, even though I hate it. At least no one who knows me will think to look for me here.

I could live in a bigger place, but this is fine. I don't want a lot of things cluttering up my life. I'm so over *things*.

My phone still sits on the floor, and the invisible heartbeat has died down. Time to call Katelyn.

Time to call off the date.

I pick up the phone. It's no longer icy. I'm back in my right mind. I was always in my right mind. Everything else was imagined because, as much as I *know* I need to call it off, I absolutely do not want to.

But I will.

I pull up Katelyn's number and hit call.

One ring. Two. Three. Then,

"Hello."

Her voice. Soft and sweet and innocent. No way was the woman ever an escort.

I clear my throat. "Good morning...Katelyn. This is Luke Johnson. From last night."

A minor pause. "Hi, Luke. How are you?"

"I'm...fine. Getting ready to hit the gym." Like she cares.

Why did I say that? It's not even true. Hitting the gym for me is putting on a Yankees hat and jogging in the park. I can't actually go to a real gym. It's too risky.

"Oh. That's nice."

Yeah, this is going well. "Hey, Katelyn, it turns out that…"

"Yes?"

"It turns out that…" I inhale. *Do it. Just do it.* "It turns out that I couldn't get a reservation for the restaurant I wanted for our dinner tonight."

"Oh. I'm sorry to hear that."

"So…you know. I was thinking…"

"Yeah?"

I made a mistake. I can't keep our date. It's not the right time for me.

My God, I'm being ridiculous. The words are right on the tip of my tongue, hovering there, ready to flow, but…

"I was thinking we'd try a different place."

I hit myself on the side of the head. I couldn't do it. Just couldn't. I want to see this woman again, whether or not it's a good idea.

"Sure. Okay. I'm new here so it doesn't matter to me where we go. Everything's new to me."

My heart is gunning rapid-fire.

"Okay. So I'll text you with the details. Unless you want me to come get you."

"No. No. I'll just meet you, like we decided last night."

"Okay. That's all I wanted to say."

"All right, Luke. Thanks."

Thanks? For what? For making a complete idiot out of myself?

I'm acting like I've never spoken to a woman before, when in fact…

Except all of that was then.

All of this is now.

"Bye, Katelyn."

"Bye."

I cover my head with the Yankees cap. I don't even follow baseball.

My shirt is long-sleeved. It's fall, of course, and I haven't yet begun the tattoo laser removal process. What if someone recognizes the ink? Until I can find someone I trust to do the job, I need to cover my left arm. Even in warm weather, I wear long sleeves.

It sucks.

But it is what it is.

I drop to the floor and rattle off a hundred pushups.

Then I shove my phone and my wallet into the pocket of my sweatpants, and I'm off.

13

KATELYN

I spend the rest of the day on my laptop, searching for and applying for work. I'm not qualified to do anything. The escort lie that I told Luke came off the top of my head. I was hardly an escort on the island. I was property.

Growing up in LA, I learned all about escort services. My mother even worked as an escort for a few years. That's how she met my father.

She claims she never had sex with her clients. For a long time, I believed her.

Now? I'm not so sure.

My phone buzzes.

So strange. It's my mother. She always seems to call me when I'm thinking about her. Kismet? Or just bad-ass luck?

"Hi, Mom," I say into the phone.

"Hi, honey. I'm just checking in."

"You checked in two days ago," I say dryly.

I don't mean to be rude to her. I don't. But I was gone for nearly a decade. They stopped looking for me. They assumed I was dead.

I shouldn't blame them. They never could have found me anyway. The only reason the island was exposed was because the owner, Derek Wolfe, was murdered and all of his kids were implicated. They fought hard to prove their innocence, leaving no stones unturned. One of those stones turned out to be Treasure Island.

Derek Wolfe was an interesting man. He helped train the women before they came to the island, but he never hunted us or violated us at the actual island. Yet he facilitated others to do so.

He had two soft spots. Diamond, our "housemother," and his daughter, Riley Wolfe.

Riley came to the island sometimes. Every once in a while I or one of the other women would catch sight of her.

All that time, Derek Wolfe never touched any of us...but he was doing unspeakable things to his own daughter.

Acid pools in my mouth.

"Baby, Dad and I really want you to come home."

"We've been through this, Mom."

"But we missed so much of your life. And you need to be with people who love you."

"I need to be alone for now. We've been through this," I say again.

"We know what you're going through."

I hate those words. I *hate* those fucking words so much. My mother has no idea what I'm going through. She thinks she does, but unless you've been held captive, tortured, raped, and hunted, you don't know.

Sorry, you just don't.

"Mom, please. You don't."

"Well...not specifically, but you know I've been through..."

I tune her out.

Her mother spanked her. Her daddy wasn't there for her.

Blah, blah, blah.

Life is rough when you're born into the upper middle class in LA. So rough that you find work as a high-paid escort and snag a tech millionaire from Brooklyn.

Blah, blah, blah.

I move the phone away from my ear and hit speaker. My mother will jabber for another two or three minutes before I can even attempt to get a word in.

While she's yammering, I get a text. From Luke.

Seven p.m. at Biscotti's. Can't wait to see you.

My heart skips a beat.

What have I gotten into?

I shouldn't be having feelings for anyone, especially not some man I just met.

I should never have let that kiss happen.

But oh...how I want to experience it again.

Maybe I can still catch Macy. It's nearly noon. She said she's here every morning. Does that mean she leaves at noon? Or has she already left?

It's worth a shot.

"Mom," I say.

Farrah continues yammering.

"Mom."

"Mom."

"Mom!"

Finally she stops talking. "Yes, Katelyn?"

"I'm really sorry, but I have an appointment, and I'm running late."

"Oh...of course."

I'm not immune to the soft scoff in her voice. She's put off that something else might be more important than talking to her.

And she wonders why I don't want to go home to LA?

I roll my eyes.

"I'll talk to you soon," I say. "Love you. Bye." I click off the phone, shove it in the pocket of my jeans, grab all my keys, and head downstairs.

As I walk off the elevator, I spy Macy walking toward the building entrance.

Shit. She's leaving. I guess it can wait—

"Macy!" I call.

I'm surprised at myself. This isn't my way. I never take this kind of initiative.

Macy turns. "Katelyn, is everything all right?"

"Yeah. Yeah. I think so."

"You *think* so?"

"Do you..." I clear my throat. "Do you have a minute?"

"Of course." She walks toward me. "You want to go into my office?"

"Yes, thank you."

I follow Macy back into the fellowship hall and through a door behind the wall. Her office is small but cozy. A photo of two children and two dogs hangs on the wall.

"Yours?"

"Guilty," she says. "Two babies and two fur babies."

"They're beautiful."

"Thank you. I like them." She smiles. "What can I do for you, Katelyn?"

"I... Well... I kind of have a date tonight."

Macy widens her eyes. "Oh?"

"Yeah. It's... Well, I was at The Glass House with Zee last night."

"When she went into labor?"

"Yeah. How are she and the baby, by the way?"

"I haven't heard anything since Reid's text this morning, but I assume everything's good." She grabs her phone. "Here's a photo."

I take the phone from her. Zee's face is pale and her eyes rimmed with dark circles, and baby Honor is a red newborn.

But I don't think I've ever seen anything so beautiful in my life.

A smile splits my face before I know it.

"A new baby puts things into perspective, doesn't it?" Macy says.

I nod. I have no words. I never thought I'd have a baby. I never thought I'd live this long. Now...is it all possible?

"The thing you said today during group," I say, "that you don't have to wait until life is no longer difficult to be happy."

She nods.

"Those words... They spoke to me. I've been through the wringer and hung out to dry. So much therapy, and it helped, of course. I wouldn't be here, on my own—well, sort of on my own—if it hadn't worked. But Macy, during all that therapy, no one ever said those particular words."

"Really?"

"Really. And they seem so simple."

"Life is far from simple, Katelyn," Macy says, "but in the end, happiness is a choice. You can choose to be miserable, or you can choose to be happy. Unfortunately, many choose the former."

"Do you think... Do you think I could have chosen happiness on the island?"

Macy smiles. "Now that's a different thing altogether. You were being abused, kept against your will. There's only so much a good attitude can do for a person. My words were meant for your life *now*. I was particularly responding to Lily's comment that she expects to be happy someday. In my mind, there's no reason for her to wait until someday. She's no longer being held against her will. She's no longer being hunted and violated. She's free. There's no reason for happiness to be left for someday. Does that make sense to you?"

"It does."

"Was that all? Or did you want to talk about something else?"

"I... Yeah... I want to talk about something else, but I don't want to keep you."

"You're not keeping me. I'm here to help, Katelyn."

"I know, but you said you're here in the mornings."

"I am. Eight until noon. But I don't have anything pressing, so I'm glad to stay a few moments to help you."

"Thank you. That's kind of you."

"Being a therapist is a twenty-four-seven thing," she says.

"What do you do in the afternoons?"

"I have a private practice."

I nod. "Okay."

"My first appointment isn't until two o'clock today, so I have some time to chat with you. What's troubling you, Katelyn?"

"Nothing," I say, "which I think is the issue."

She smiles. "You're going to have to elaborate."

The story spills out of me. Luke. His kisses. Our date tonight. His earlier phone call, which was odd.

"And how are you feeling about this date?" Macy asks.

"I'm ambivalent," I tell her. "Totally ambivalent. I'm excited about it. Truly. I'm attracted to this man. But on the other hand, I have no business putting myself out there yet.

I'm so far from a whole person. I've been through literal hell, Macy. I don't know what to do."

"What do you *want* to do?"

"I want to go."

"Then go. You've done your due diligence. You're meeting him there. You're not going to be alone with him. Not unless you choose it. *You* have the power, Katelyn."

"I'm not used to having the power."

"I know you're not. But you said this morning in group that you kept your name because you wanted to take it back. You wanted to take back your life. This is all part of that."

I nod. She's right. Everything she says makes perfect and logical sense.

So why am I fighting it?

"I just met him," I say, "and I let him kiss me."

"Do you feel you could have stopped him?"

"Yes. Yes, I do. He wasn't at all forceful."

"Then you kissed him because you wanted to. True, you may not be completely ready for any kind of relationship, but stepping out of the comfort zone isn't a bad thing."

"Except...I don't feel like I stepped out of my comfort zone," I say. "Kissing Luke felt... It felt...completely normal. Completely wonderful. I wasn't even scared."

"Not at all?"

"Only of the fact that I wasn't scared. If that makes any kind of twisted sense."

"Yes, it does make sense," Macy says. "We all heal in our own individual way, Katelyn. What works for Lily or anyone else may not work for you. You have an inner strength that I don't see in some of the other women."

"I do? I don't feel strong at all."

"But you are. I've read your file from the center. I know

how you found your strength—your will to live—while you were captive. That's something so amazing. Don't ever doubt that you can make the right decisions for you. You have that strength. That intelligence. You have drive, Katelyn. Drive to succeed, and that's why you *will* be whole again. You're nearly there already."

Nearly there already?

That's a stretch.

A real stretch.

I don't reply to Macy's comment.

Instead, I say, "Thank you for staying late for me."

"I hope to see you next time at group, Katelyn. Or if you want to make an appointment for a private session, I'm always available."

I nod.

And I smile.

Macy believes in me.

Or she makes a good show of it.

14

LUKE

Biscotti's isn't The Glass House. It's less expensive, for one, which *should* be a consideration for me but it's not. It is, however, less visible, which is *always* a consideration for me.

Someone who needs to lie low shouldn't be taking the most beautiful woman in Manhattan to dinner.

But someone can't help himself.

What I'm feeling is different.

No longer am I a slave to beautiful women or to my own desires. No. I want to *see* Katelyn. Talk to her. Learn about her. Get to know her.

Sure, if I'm honest, I'd love to take her to bed and screw her senseless. I'm still a guy, after all.

But I know I won't.

I'm different now. I can do this the right way. Even though I shouldn't be doing it at all.

I wait outside the restaurant. I could go in and tell the maître d' that I'm here, but I want to go in as a couple.

I twist my lips and lean against the building as people

scurry by. Just another Manhattan evening. Everyone's in a hurry here. Always rushing. Taxis honk as they weave through traffic. If it's possible, this traffic is even worse than LA. At least there are highways that go through LA. Here? It's all congestion all the time.

I hate it.

But big cities are all I know.

I'm wearing black pants and a black button-down. No tie. Easy attire, and easy to blend in. I scan the crowds scurrying up and down the street, looking for a particular blond head.

Is she coming? Will she stand me up? Give me the rabbit, as the French say?

My heart races faster. What if she does? What if she stands me up? It might be the best thing for both of us, but I may die an untimely death if I can't see her again.

Still, I do know where she lives...

But I'm not that guy anymore. I made a promise to myself.

If I ever do it again, I'll do it right.

Damn. Where is she?

If she doesn't show, I'll deal. Not like I have a choice. I won't go back to my previous bad habits. I don't want to be that person anymore.

Besides, if I do, my life will be over.

I grab my phone out of my pocket. She never acknowledged my text, but she also didn't say she *wouldn't* be here.

Did she even get the text? It says delivered, but what if her phone is dead? Or she's separated from her phone. Or the cell tow—

She's there then. In front of me. Her lips curved slightly upward, her gorgeous blond locks swept off her shoulders into a messy bun.

She wears a pink camisole—damn, I can see her nipples

through the silky fabric—and black skinny jeans. Simple patent leather pumps with a medium heel. No jewelry other than plain gold studs in her pierced ears.

She's utterly beautiful.

"Katelyn," I say, my voice coming out breathy.

Get a grip, for God's sake.

"Hi, Luke."

"I'm glad you came."

"Did you think I wouldn't?"

"You didn't text me back."

She widens her eyes. "Was I supposed to? After you called, you said you'd text, so I just..."

"It's okay. You're here now." I pull open the door of the restaurant and gesture to her.

She walks in and then stops.

She wants me to take the lead. Okay. That's cool. The reservation is in my name anyway. I proceed to the maître d'.

"May I help you, sir?"

"Yes. I have a reservation for two. Johnson."

Johnson. The name still feels strange coming off my tongue.

Luke isn't nearly as strange. Maybe because everyone calls me that daily. No one calls me Johnson.

"Yes, Mr. Johnson." The maître d' makes a mark on an iPad. "You're table's ready." He hands off two menus to a young woman. "Loretta will show you to your table."

"Thank you." I gesture to Katelyn to follow Loretta.

She does, which gives me a bird's-eye view of her perfect ass. The satin of her untucked camisole clings to every curve.

My dick responds, but I tamp down the desire. Not the place. Not the time. Who knows when the time or place will be? In normal circumstances, it might be tonight at my place.

These are not normal circumstances.

I hold out a chair for Katelyn. Her cheeks go pink as she takes a seat and arranges her napkin on her lap. Loretta hands her a menu.

"Thank you," Katelyn murmurs.

"You're most welcome. David will be taking care of you tonight. He'll be with you soon."

"Thank you, Loretta," I say.

Always use a person's name, if you know it. My mother taught me that.

Seems like a lifetime ago. In many ways, it was.

"Would you like a drink?" I ask Katelyn.

"I don't know. Maybe."

"Whatever you want," I tell her. "Order the most expensive thing on the menu if you'd like."

She blushes further. "I'd never do that."

"I want you to. I want you to have your heart's desire."

Where are these words coming from? They're foreign, but no less true. As I stare at the angelic beauty across from me, I want to give her happiness.

Happiness doesn't come from things, though. I learned that lesson the hard way, and I'll do well to remember it. That's what got me into trouble in the first place. Well...that and my drinking.

"Good evening."

I look to my left. Our waiter, presumably, stands here.

"I'm David and I'm happy to be serving you this evening. Would either of you care for a cocktail?"

"Katelyn?" I say.

She gives a light smile but doesn't look at David. "I'd like a lemon drop."

"Wonderful choice. And you, sir?"

"Just sparkling water with lime, please."

"Very good. Do you have any questions about the menu?"

"I haven't had a chance to look yet."

"Me neither," Katelyn says.

"Good enough. I'll get these drinks for you right away."

Katelyn opens her menu. "No drink for you?"

"Sparkling water's a drink last time I checked." I grin.

"You know what I mean."

"I'm a recovering alcoholic," I say.

"Oh... I'm sorry."

"Why?"

She laughs lightly. "Honestly? I guess I just assumed you had trouble when you drank. I'm sorry. I shouldn't have made that assumption."

She's so on target. "I got into a lot of trouble when I drank, so you're right. But it was all my own doing. No reason for you to be sorry."

"How long have you been clean?"

"Just a few months."

Her eyes widen.

"You were expecting it be longer?"

"I suppose I was. Good for you. Has it been difficult?"

More than you can imagine. "I take it one day at a time."

"Would you rather I not have a drink?"

"Of course not. I work at a restaurant, as you know. I serve alcohol. I can't expect the world to revolve around me."

True story, and a major hurdle I had to overcome.

I look back and can't even believe the person I was just a short time ago. What a fucking mess.

"I don't drink that much," Katelyn says. "I thought a cocktail might be a good idea tonight, though."

"Oh? Why?"

"To take the edge off."

"Do I frighten you, Katelyn?"

She smiles. God, she's gorgeous.

"No, you don't. But that frightens me."

I return her smile. In a bizarre way, I get what she's saying. I shouldn't be here either, but I'm drawn to her. She's basically saying that I have the same effect on her.

Which is cool. Really cool. And as she says, a little frightening.

What's her story?

I can't ask her, or she'll want mine. I still don't believe she was ever an escort in LA or anywhere else. She's not the right type. Not even close.

Katelyn looks down at her menu, and I feel a loss when her gaze shifts.

"You don't frighten me, either," I say.

"Of course I don't."

"What's that mean?"

"It means you're a guy. Guys don't have to be frightened of women."

Actually, they do, albeit for different reasons. At least *I* have reasons to be frightened of women.

But Katelyn doesn't frighten me.

She intrigues me.

She's different from most women.

In my previous life, women fell all over me.

Now? I still get a fair amount of attention, but Katelyn's so different.

She's not a flirt. She's not a talker.

God, she so was *not* an escort. Without flirting and talking, an escort will be out of business in no time flat.

Before we can converse further, David returns with our

drinks. "Lemon drop for the lady." He sets the martini glass full of clear liquid in front of Katelyn. "And sparkling water with lime. Would you like to order an appetizer? Our calamari is excellent."

I love calamari. "That sounds good. Katelyn?"

"I don't eat seafood," she says.

Damn, I'm a moron. She said the same last night.

"Maybe the crispy brussels sprouts," Katelyn offers.

I smile. "Perfect. Calamari for me and brussels sprouts for the lady."

"Of course." David makes a note on his pad. "The chef has two specials tonight. One is a lobster macaroni and cheese, and it's out of this world. The other is a New York strip with gorgonzola butter, which is served with broccoli rabe and a side of spaghetti marinara."

"Thanks," I say. "They sound great. We'll need a few more minutes."

"Not a problem. I'll get your appetizers going." He leaves swiftly.

"Lobster mac and cheese?" Katelyn says.

"I know. It's kind of champagne meets beer. But I have to admit it sounds pretty good."

"I love macaroni and cheese," she says. "It was my favorite growing up."

"You should try it."

"I don't normally eat seafood."

"Right. I remember that from last night. I'm sorry I suggested the calamari. Are you allergic?"

"No, no. I just... For a while I was for— I mean, I ate a lot of it, so now I'm kind of over it."

I lift my eyebrows. An interesting answer. "How about the

steak special, then? Wait. Never mind. You don't eat red meat."

Her eyes shine. "You have a good memory."

"It was only last night. I have to tell you, though. I'm surprised about the seafood thing. You being from Cali and all."

She blushes slightly. "I guess I got sick of it."

"I get it. You ate a lot of it growing up and now you're over it."

"Yeah. That's about right."

There's a story there, but I won't push it. I want this to work, which means I must go slow. That means not pushing for information. I'll let her volunteer it.

It also means not pushing things physically.

That will be the harder of the two.

Except it's not, so far.

I want more information. I want to know this woman, and not just in the biblical sense.

I want to know about her childhood, about her hobbies, about what she likes to read. What plays she's seen. What she likes to binge-watch.

I'm not a binge-watcher myself, but I do like old sitcoms. *Friends* and *Will and Grace* are two of my favorites.

"Katelyn," I say, "what do you li—"

Katelyn's mouth drops open, and her eyes go wide.

She's not looking at me.

She's looking past me.

Something grips the back of my neck. I can feel her fear as if it's my own.

15

KATELYN

I ce Man comes to see me every other month. He looks past all the other women and zeroes in on me.

He doesn't hunt me. He doesn't physically hurt me.

But he's a master at humiliation.

I never meet his gaze.

I always hope that this time, he'll decide to try another woman.

He never does.

"Moonstone," he says in his gravelly voice.

"Good evening." I don't look up.

"Say my name," he commands.

I clear my throat. If I don't, I may not be able to say anything. "Mr. Smith."

It's not his real name. A lot of Mr. Smiths come to the island. A lot of Mr. Browns and Mr. Joneses. A few Mr. Warners and Mr. Tylers. One Mr. Kovich.

But to me, this Mr. Smith is Ice Man.

I should probably be happy he's here. I won't be beaten tonight. I won't be hunted. I won't be cut or hurt physically in any way.

Instead, I'll be told what a disgusting slut I am, how I deserve to be treated like shit. And then I'll be urinated on. Ice Man will freeze what's left of his urine into cubes. At least he doesn't make me use those cubes in my drink. He uses them himself.

All fetishes are allowed here on Treasure Island, no matter how disgusting.

That's what Ice Man likes to do.

Here on Treasure Island, nothing is off limits. Except killing. They can't kill us. They can, however, bring us to the brink of death. I've seen it happen. Sapphire was out of commission for two months when a visitor broke her leg. Crystal was out for longer than that after a visitor burned her breasts. She's scarred for life now, but she's still expected to entertain visitors. Even with her burn scars, she's still one of the most beautiful women here, and she never lacks for company. Some men like the scars—another fetish.

How I wish I lacked for company.

Sapphire and Crystal would probably be happy to entertain Ice Man.

But physical pain isn't the only kind of pain.

Mental pain—humiliation—is also pain.

And I don't want it. Not tonight. Not ever.

"Come with me, Moonstone." *Mr. Smith holds out his hand to me.*

Mr. Smith always wears a mask over his eyes. Still, I know it's him. His eyes are a light brown, almost golden—ironically close to the color of the bodily fluid he's obsessed with.

I'll never forget those eyes.

No matter how much I want to.

~

No.

No.

He can't be here.

Didn't they arrest everyone who frequented the island? Shouldn't he be rotting in prison somewhere?

Ice Man.

Those eyes.

They're forever embedded in my brain as if they were branded there with a hot iron.

My therapist at the retreat center hypothesized that Ice Man hated his fetish as much as or more than he craved it, which is why, after using his bodily fluid to humiliate me, he then used it to humiliate himself with the ice cubes. Maybe and maybe not. Either way, I don't give a damn about his supposed self-hatred any other problems he undoubtedly has —and I'm sure there are many.

He humiliated me, abused me, and I don't want him anywhere near me ever again.

I bury my head in my menu, not bothering to commit the rest of his appearance to memory.

"Katelyn?" Luke says.

I say nothing.

I can't talk. Can't look. Can't do anything to alert Ice Man that I'm here.

He walks closer, walks by our table.

I allow myself to breathe out slightly in relief—

"Have we met?"

I go numb. That's why he's Ice Man. Not just because he freezes his urine, but because he turns me to ice.

It's his voice. His eyes. His very essence.

I say nothing.

"Have we met?" he says again.

"Can I help you?" Luke looks up and meets Iceman's gaze.

"I was speaking to the lady."

"Katelyn?" Luke says.

"Katelyn. Is that your name now?"

"Now?" Luke asks.

"You've mistaken me for someone else," I say, still hiding behind the menu.

"Excuse me," Luke says, "but we're trying to have dinner here."

"I mean no disrespect," Ice Man says.

Yeah. Right.

"I'm sure we've met," he continues. "Maybe on…vacation? In the tropics?"

The tropics. The island. He has to mention it. Sickness wells in me, but I gulp it down. "I don't think so."

"I'm sure we have."

"The lady says you're mistaken," Luke says.

"The lady is the one who's mistaken."

Luke stands then. He's taller than Ice Man but with a slightly leaner build. "Take a hint. She's with me."

"For now." Ice Man saunters away, as cool and confident as ever.

I assume he takes a seat at another table. I don't know. I don't have eyes in the back of my head, and I don't dare turn around.

"Katelyn," Luke says as he takes his seat across from me.

"I don't know him."

"I believe you." Though his words lack truth. I can tell by his tone. He doesn't sound harsh or anything. But still I know.

He doesn't believe me.

Why should he? I'm lying.

"Hey." He gently removes my menu from my hands. "It's okay."

It's not okay. How can it be okay? My past is coming back to haunt me. My past that I thought I was finally free of.

Ice Man can't hurt me. He wouldn't dare. Would he?

Maybe he's changed.

No, he hasn't. Once a sicko always a sicko.

"Can we go?" I ask Luke.

"Uh...yeah. Sure. Let me pay for the drinks and—"

"Okay. I'll wait for you outside. I need to... I need to..." I rise.

Can't breathe. Can't even see.

Where's the exit? Where's the...

Images blur around me. I clutch the edge of the table to keep from losing my footing.

Luke stands abruptly and grips my shoulders. "Katelyn. Baby. Talk to me."

"I need to get out of here. Please."

He stares at me. Gazes into my eyes. I don't know what he sees, but whatever it is, it spurs him into action. He places his arm around my waist and guides me toward the front of the restaurant.

He stops for a second to tell the maître d' that he'll be back in to take care of the drink bill, and then he directs me out the door and onto the sidewalk.

I melt into his arms.

If not for his solid form, I'd be crumpled on the hard sidewalk.

"Baby, baby," he murmurs into my hair. "What is it? Who is that?"

"No one," I lie. "I don't know him."

"He seems to know you." He grips my shoulders once

more and moves me backward just enough so that our eyes meet. "What did that man do to you?"

What a loaded question.

And it's one I can't answer.

Not now.

Not ever.

16

LUKE

She's shivering. It's not a cold night, but Katelyn shivers against me. I rub her back, trying to ease her chill.

The bill. I have to go back in and take care of the drink bill.

"Hey," I say against her ear. "Will you be okay? I just have to close out our bill."

"No. Don't leave me."

"I'll be right back. They're going to come after me if I don't."

She pulls back. "Okay. Okay," she chokes out. "Just hurry. Please."

"I will." I kiss the top of her head. "Stay right here. Don't move."

She nods as I head back into the restaurant.

And who do I run right into?

The jerk who's bothering her. Man, this guy has yellow eyes. Who the hell has eyes that color?

"Where do you think *you're* going?" I demand.

"To get some air."

"No." I stand in front of him.

"You can move," he says, "or I can move you."

"I'd like to see you try."

Yeah. It's all coming back to me. My life on the streets. The way to get someone to back down isn't to *be* tougher. It's to *act* tougher.

I can do both. This guy's got ten years on me. I can take him.

Fuck. I don't want to go back to who I was, but Katelyn... This man bothers Katelyn.

He raises a hand. I block him.

"What the hell's going on there?" From the maître d'.

I quickly pull out a twenty and throw it toward him. It flutters to the floor. "For my drinks." Then I grab the asshole and push him out the door.

And nearly into Katelyn.

She gasps and leans against the building for support. "Luke..."

"Don't worry. This creep won't bother you ever again." I meet his loathsome gaze. "Will you?"

"I have no intention of bothering her." Then he glares at her. "But I will see you again...*Katelyn*."

That's it. I don't give a fuck. I push the bastard into the brick wall and grab him by the throat, my heart pounding. "She doesn't like you, man. Leave her alone."

"She used to like me a lot."

"She doesn't now. Get lost."

"I'll have you arrested for assault."

"It's battery, dumbass, and no you won't."

"The cops are already on their way. I called 911 before I left the restaurant."

He's bluffing. Already I know this jerk doesn't want the

cops anywhere near him. I know his type. "Great. Then my lady friend here will be happy to tell them how you're stalking her."

Then I can't help myself. I chuckle, because who do I see coming toward us but a beat cop walking the street.

Nice. Maybe he *did* call the cops, though I doubt it.

This guy looks like a normal beat cop. He's not in a hurry...until he sees that I'm holding a guy by the throat.

"Trouble, fellas?" he says when he approaches.

"Nah. Just keeping a stalker in line," I say.

"Oh?"

"Yeah. He's bothering my dinner companion."

"Out here?"

"He was inside the restaurant."

"Let him go, man."

I release my hold on Yellow Eyes's throat. He loosens his tie, gasping softly.

"I need to see some ID, please," the cop says to me.

"Am I under arrest?"

"I'm not sure yet. ID, please."

"Officer," Katelyn interrupts, "Luke didn't do anything wrong. This man was bothering me."

"I'll take your statement in a moment, ma'am. ID"—the cop glances at Yellow Eyes—"both of you."

I pull out my wallet, extract my New York driver's license, and hand it to Officer Lydeck, as his badge indicates.

"Mr. Johnson," Lydeck says. "Very good. And yours, sir."

Yellow Eyes glares at me as he opens his wallet and pulls out his ID.

"Mr. Pollack," Lydeck says, "you're a long way from home."

Yellow Eyes—Pollack—rubs at his throat. "On business," he says, his voice slightly hoarse.

Of course it was slightly hoarse before, so I doubt I did any damage.

Where the hell is he from? A long way from home could mean Buffalo or Moscow, for all I know.

"Now, who wants to tell me what the hell is going on here?" Lydeck rubs his chin.

Katelyn steps forward, looking more self-assured than I've ever seen her. Not that I've seen a lot of her, but boy, she sure looks like she's ready to raise some hell.

"Luke and I were having dinner inside," she says, "when I —I mean, this man—came by our table and tried to talk to me. Wanted to know if we'd met before. I said no, but he insisted."

"And then...?"

"He went to his table, but I was upset."

"Why would that upset you, ma'am?" Lydeck asks.

"Just the way he looked at me. It was...creepy."

"She wanted to leave," I interject. "So I walked her outside. I went back in to take care of our bill, and I ran into this creep who told me he was going outside to talk to her."

"He was?" Katelyn gasps.

"Yeah. And the lady obviously wants nothing to do with him, but he wouldn't take no for an answer, so I slammed him against the building."

"You're admitting that," Lydeck says.

"I sure as hell am, and I don't regret it. The guy's clearly a creep who's stalking a woman who wants nothing to do with him. Aren't there laws against that?"

"There are," Lydeck says. "There are also laws against assault and battery."

"I understand that, officer. But when a man bothers my dinner companion, I can't let it lie."

The officer nods and hands me my license. "It's your lucky day"—he eyes me—"Mr. Johnson." He turns to Pollack and gives him his license. "As for you, sir, leave the lady alone."

"You're not going to arrest him?" Katelyn asks.

"I can't arrest every man who tries to speak to a woman," Lydeck says. "We wouldn't have enough room at the jailhouse."

He thinks he's being funny, but there's nothing funny about this from where I'm standing.

"But when a lady says to go away," Lydeck says to Pollack, "you go away. Do you understand me?"

"I want to file charges against this character." Pollack gestures to me.

"I don't recommend that, sir," the officer retorts. "The lady says you were bothering her."

"I didn't touch her. Didn't harm her in any way. I just wanted to talk to her."

"And it's her right to refuse to talk to you," Lydeck says. "Push me any further on this, and I will arrest you."

Pollack adjusts his collar once more before placing his license back in his wallet. "Do you know who I am?"

"Do I look like I *care* who you are?" Lydeck says. "I don't give a rat's ass who you are. I care about what you *do*. You leave this lady alone, and remember that the next time you decide to talk to someone who tells you to get lost. For Christ's sake."

"I'm a married man." Pollack holds up his left hand, displaying a gawdy thick gold band. "I just thought this woman was a friend of my daughter's. I can see now I'm mistaken."

Yeah, right. And I've got some frozen tundra in Siberia I want to sell you, too. He's lying. I can spot a liar a mile away. Something that came in handy in my former life.

"Keep your distance from now on," Lydeck says to Pollack. "And you"—he turns to me, —keep your hands to yourself."

"Of course, Officer."

Right. Mess with Katelyn and I'll come after you every time.

This guy is bad news. I feel it. And I know a bad guy.

I used to be one.

17

KATELYN

I stand, numb.

I can't look into Ice Man's eyes. I can't go back to that place.

I don't mean the island. I mean the *place*. The place inside myself. The place where I'm no one.

~

"YOU MEAN SO MUCH *to these gentlemen," Diamond says. "I realize they mistreat you, but you provide something for them. Because of you, they don't mistreat the other women in their lives."*

Diamond's canned speech. How many times have I heard it now?

See, Diamond, we don't care that they're not hurting others. We care that they're hurting us.

Diamond doesn't believe her words either. They're rehearsed. It's like a teleprompter is playing in her head.

"Moonstone?" she says. "Do you have a question?"

"No."

"You were shaking your head."

"I just need an appointment," I say. *"To talk to you in private."*

"Of course. We're done here. Come with me."

I follow Diamond to her office. It's not an office so much as a sitting room that's attached to her bedroom in the dorm.

The dorm. That's what our housing unit is called. We each have our own separate room, but the men don't come here. It's off limits and heavily guarded.

Basically, we're off the clock while we're here. And if the men don't pay, they don't play.

"What's bothering you, Moonstone?"

"Your words."

"Which ones?"

"You know which ones. Diamond, you don't really believe the trash you spew, do you?"

She sighs. *"No, I don't. But that's between you and me, Moonstone."*

"It's Katelyn. You know my fucking name."

"It's not. Not anymore. I'm supposed to punish you for using your former name. But I'm not going to."

"Why?"

"Because I'm going to let you in on a little secret," she says. *"I don't like this any more than you do. I hate it. Abhor it. If I had it my way, I'd let every last one of you go."*

"Why don't you?"

"I have no choice."

"You do. There's always a choice, Diamond."

She sighs. Pauses. Sighs again. *"I have someone else I have to think about. You won't understand."*

"You're damned right I won't." I huff and walk out the door.

I was strong and feisty when I first showed up at the island. My shoulders had healed, and I wanted to fight.

They gradually broke the fight out of me, and I never questioned Diamond again.

I became Moonstone.

I hardly recalled Katelyn.

She no longer existed.

I decided I wanted to live, but it wasn't until the center that I truly found my strength again.

∼

"KEEP your distance from now on. And you, keep your hands to yourself." From the officer.

Luke isn't being arrested. I'm glad.

Neither is Ice Man. Not so glad on that part.

Granted, he didn't touch me.

But I felt unsafe.

Unsafe in his presence. Unsafe because he was near. And then he came out of the restaurant to find me again. Luckily Luke found him first.

"Next time either of you crosses my radar," the officer says, "you'll be arrested. Got it?"

"Yes, sir." Ice Man holds out his hand. "Thank you for your service."

I want to puke. Seriously puke. My stomach is cramping, and I force myself not to bend over. I breathe through the cramping.

Doesn't help.

"Ma'am," Ice Man says to me, "please accept my apologies. I never meant to frighten you. You bear a striking resemblance to a friend of my daughter's."

"Bullshit," I grit out.

Good. Good job, Katelyn. You worked through the nausea, the cramping, the raw fear. Show him you won't be intimidated.

Except now I think I might faint dead away.

"I'm sorry," he says again.

"Fuck off." This from Luke.

Officer Lydeck rolls his eyes. "Get the hell out of here. All of you."

Luke and I haven't had dinner yet, but I can't eat anyway with my stomach doing twists and turns. Ice Man walks away but then looks over his shoulder and meets my gaze.

His eyes speak volumes.

I'll be back for you, they say. *I'll be back for you.*

I lean against the building once more.

Officer Lydeck still stands next to Luke. "Now that he's gone," Lydeck says to me, "I'd like to hear more."

"There's no more." I gaze at the ground. At my shoes. At a piece of pinkish gum ground into the sidewalk.

"I'd like to hear more too, Katelyn," Luke says. "You know him, don't you?"

I shake my head.

"Katelyn..."

I meet Luke's gaze. His dark eyes are kind. Caring. I want to spill everything.

Of course, if I do that, he'll run as far away as he can from me.

The officer, though? I could tell him. I could ask him why Ice Man isn't behind bars like the others. Even Prince Christian of Cordova is in prison in his own municipality. Some things can't be forgiven.

"I don't know him," I say again.

Office Lydeck pulls out his wallet, opens it, and hands me a business card. "Anytime you want to talk, call. I'll listen.

And I'll make sure charges stick if they're warranted." He hands another card to Luke. "Just in case."

Luke nods. "Thank you. And thanks for letting the battery go."

"I know a derelict when I see one," Lydeck says. "That man may be dressed well and have ID and a wife, but he's up to no good. I hated letting him go."

"Why did you, then?" Luke asks.

"Because trying to speak to a woman isn't a crime in New York. If he'd touched her in any way, I could have done something."

"What about stalking?"

"Has he tried to contact you before?" the officer asks me.

I clear my throat. "No."

Except on the island, but that doesn't count. And I sure can't get into that on a busy Manhattan street on a weekday evening.

"If he tries again, call me. Anytime," Officer Lydeck stresses.

"Okay," I say. "Thank you."

"You're welcome. I wish I could do more. Both of you try to have a nice evening. What's left of it." He tips his hat and is on his way.

Luke turns to me then. "You want to see if I can get our table back?"

"God, no. Not in there. I'm creeped out."

"Katelyn."

"Hmm?"

"You *do* know him."

A statement. Not a question. Luke already knows, so why deny it?

"I do. He was...a client when I was an escort." Nice lie. Believable, at least.

"And did he...?"

"Hurt me? No." Not physically, anyway. Heck, he didn't even fuck me. He was one of the easier visitors.

But he was my least favorite.

I scoff silently. Least favorite? Such a misnomer. It sounds like I actually had a favorite, which I didn't. They all were horrible satanic people.

They all deserve to burn in hell.

"What is it, then?" Luke asks.

"He's a creep. A bona fide creep."

"Did he ever stalk you?"

I don't reply. The answer is both yes and no. Yes, in that he always came back to me on the island. But no. In reality, he never stalked me. The island was far from reality.

"Katelyn. Please. Answer me."

"No. Not really. I just don't like him. I left that part of my life in LA."

Luke trails a finger over my forearm. Just a light touch, but I shiver.

"Are you ever going to level with me?" he asks.

"About what?"

"About your past. I know you weren't an escort."

"Sure, I was." It's not even a lie. I'm simply making the truth more palatable.

"Katelyn... I'm originally from LA, remember? I know how escort services work. The women are talkative, flirty."

"Maybe I used to be talkative and flirty." Not a lie. I was. Before.

Before I was taken.

Before I was forced into prostitution.

Before I was forced into the hunt.

"Were you?" he asks. "And if you were, why did you change?"

I don't answer.

I *can't* answer.

"I'm no longer hungry," I say. "I want to go home."

Luke reaches toward me again but then hesitates and pulls his hand back to his side. "All right. If that's what you want."

Is it? Is it what I want? I don't have a fucking clue what I actually want. I like this man. I shouldn't, but I do. He's kind to me. He's gentle. I feel safe with him.

I never thought I'd feel safe with a man again.

I breathe in, hold it a few seconds, and then let the air whoosh out of my lungs in a sigh. "Luke?"

"Yeah?"

"I don't want to go home yet."

"You changed your mind that quickly?"

I nod. "I want to...walk. I need to work off some energy."

I know a better way to work off energy.

Every guy in the world would say those words, and I wait, expecting them to tumble out of Luke's mouth.

"A walk," he says instead. "It's a nice night. Okay. But we have to stop somewhere for a slice, because you may not be hungry but I'm starved. It took a hell of a lot of energy for me to *not* knock that creep unconscious."

"I wish you had." No lie there.

"Then the good officer probably wouldn't have let me go."

"True. Let me rephrase that. I wish you had and not gotten arrested."

"Better. Though if he'd touched you, he wouldn't be walking right now."

Yeah, he touched me. With his bodily fluids. With his slimy hands. But I can't go there.

Instead—

I smile.

And it's a big smile. A smile like I haven't smiled in years. It's also forced.

Luke smiles too. A huge and happy grin that splits his handsome face. "Damn, you're beautiful. You should smile like that more often."

As if he waved a magic wand, my forced smile becomes a real smile.

"Maybe I will," I say coyly.

And I already know I will, as long as Luke is in my life.

18

LUKE

We walk, not touching in any way but still close together, through the streets of Manhattan. People glide past us briskly. Everyone's always in such a hurry in New York. I miss that about LA. It's much more casual there.

But there are many more things I don't miss.

My old life, for one.

Man, I was a mess.

I have lots of red on my ledger, but there's nothing I can do about it now. I can never return to LA.

My hand brushes Katelyn's, and sparks ignite across my skin. Just that simple touch of our pinkies.

I brush against her again, and this time, she—*she*—clasps her pinky around my own.

Pinkies entwined. Just our fucking pinkies. And I'm elated. Totally elated.

I promised myself. Promised myself I wouldn't get involved with a woman so soon. Not after...

The injury to my shoulder aches. Nothing I can't handle.

Just a dull ache. It happens when I think about my previous life. When I dwell on what I was.

People can change. I know that now.

Everything I've done in my life has brought me to this place. Here. With Katelyn. Our pinkies entwined.

Was it worth it? I harmed so many...

One of my favorite pizza vendors is in the distance. "Sure I can't tempt you with a slice?" I ask.

"Maybe," she says. "But those New York pizza slices are so big."

"True. You fold them over and make your own calzone."

She giggles softly. "They're easier to eat that way, but they're still huge."

"True enough." We reach the vendor. "Hey, Sly."

"Good to see you!" That's what Sly always says.

He's here at his pizza stand from noon to nine each day, selling slices of the best pizza I've ever tasted out of his truck. I'm not sure he knows my name or anyone's. But it's always "good to see you!"

"You too. Two pepperoni slices."

"You got it." He pulls the slices onto tissue. Already the grease has saturated the paper. Good stuff.

"I'll never be able to eat all of that," Katelyn says.

"Sure you can." Sly winks. "Never met any New Yorker who couldn't put away a slice of Sly's. Even the skinniest models."

"I guess we'll see." I hand Katelyn her slice, grab about twenty napkins—and I'm still not sure that will be enough— and then pay Sly. "Thanks, man."

"Anytime, anytime."

Holding our pizza, we walk to a bench and take a seat. I push several napkins into Katelyn's hands while oil drips from the tissue paper. "Careful. You don't want to get grease on your clothes.

She takes the napkins and arranges them around her slice. "I'll never eat all of this. I'm not even hungry. Remember?"

But I see the tell. She closes her eyes and inhales. The sweet zing of the tomato sauce and the spicy garlic, the cheese, the fresh bread.

Yeah, she's going to eat.

I take a bite, and—

"Ach! Careful. It's hot." I chew quickly and swallow. "I'd wait a minute."

"It doesn't feel hot in my hand."

"It's hot in my mouth. I think I burned off a layer of my tongue."

She laughs.

"Is that funny?"

"No. Just the way you say it. I like laughing with you. Is that weird?"

"Not in the slightest. I like to hear you laugh. It's an amazing, joyful sound."

"Is it? For a while, I didn't laugh much."

I'm not surprised. Katelyn has a backstory. I'm convinced of it. And not all of it is pretty. Hell, my backstory sucks too. Maybe we're meant for each other. Maybe she can handle my baggage and I can handle hers.

Or maybe we can just enjoy a slice of New York's finest and then entwine our pinkies again.

Odd that I can get more out of pinky touching with Katelyn than I got out of my last relationship.

And man, I thought I was in love. I thought she was the one.

I was wrong.

But it wasn't her fault. It was my own. I didn't know what I wanted or how to get it.

I was fucked up.

I can blame my parents, my childhood, my circumstances.

But I don't.

Not anymore.

I want to be better. I want to be worthy.

I want to deserve this woman sitting next to me.

Someday, perhaps, I will.

I take another bite. This one is hot but not scalding. And delicious. "Try it now," I say after swallowing.

Katelyn takes a tentative bite of her pizza that's she's folded over like an expert. Her eyes widen.

"Good?"

She nods enthusiastically as she chews and swallows. "Oh my God, it's amazing!"

"Told you."

I finish my slice in record time, and Katelyn manages to eat most of hers. When she hands me what's left—mostly crust—I polish that off too.

"What now?" I ask. "You want to walk some more?"

"I need some water."

"Yeah, me too. I'm not sure what I was thinking, not getting drinks from Sly. Come on." I rise and hold out my hand.

She takes it, and tingles shoot through me. Something about this woman's hands...

I grab her trash from her and throw it in the nearby waste receptacle. Then we walk.

And I realize where I'm headed.

Twenty minutes later, we're in front of my building.

19

KATELYN

atelyn..." Luke says.

"Yeah?"

"This is where I live."

It's a tall building composed of red brick. How long have we been walking? We were supposed to get something to drink.

"Oh?"

"Yeah. Honestly, I didn't mean to come here. We were just walking, and..."

"We weren't talking."

"No. Not really. I don't want you to think that..."

"That you brought me here for sex."

"Right. That. I don't want you to think...*that*."

"I don't."

To my surprise, I find my words are true. I don't believe he brought me here for sex.

"Let me get you a cab." He walks toward the street and raises his hand.

A yellow cab stops.

"Here you go," Luke says.

Except I'm not ready to leave yet. I want to stay with Luke. I want to be with him. I don't want anything else. No sex, of course.

But I want...

I want another of his soft kisses.

I don't know how to ask for anything I want, though, so I smile weakly and slide into the back seat when Luke opens the door of the cab for me.

I meet his gaze as the cab lurches forward.

And Luke gets smaller and smaller.

This isn't what I wanted.

This isn't what I wanted at all.

~

VISITING my cousins in Brooklyn is always fun. They live in a large brownstone, on the upper floor. It gets so hot in the summer, but we didn't mind when we were kids. The second floor is enormous, and we also played outside in the cobbled streets, wishing for a fire hydrant to burst open. It happened once or twice each summer, and I always loved it when it happened during my week-long visits.

I just turned eighteen, and I was heading to the airport to fly to New York for a week. A week at the brownstone with my cousins. Sure, most of my friends were beach bumming in LA, but there was something about Brooklyn in the summer that called to me.

Maybe just because it was different.

I'm too old now to run across the cobblestones splashing around the fire hydrants. Too old to play stickball in the street.

But still I love Brooklyn.

Jared and Anthony aren't my actual cousins. They're second cousins. Our grandfathers were brothers. I have no siblings or actual cousins, as my parents are both only children.

I love Jared and Tony like they're my brothers, though. Plus, there's something about the kids in Brooklyn.

They're happy. They don't care if there's nothing to do except play stickball in the street. They're real.

I looked forward to the week at the brownstone every summer. Until I turned fourteen. Then I got a job as a lifeguard and I stayed home that summer and the next two. My last summer before college, Mom asked me if I'd like to go see Aunt Agnes and the boys.

I jumped at the chance.

This time, I'm older. A legal adult. Jared's sixteen, and Tony's seventeen. No stickball and no fire hydrants. In fact, I don't see much of Jared and Tony anymore. I hang with Aunt Agnes and I read a lot of books.

In the fall, I'll begin college at Columbia, and I'll probably see Aunt Agnes and the boys a lot on holidays. Much easier to go to Brooklyn than to get all the way across the country to LA. I'll still go home for the summers, though. As much as I love the weeks in Brooklyn, I love a summer on the beach more.

Aunt Agnes makes spaghetti and meatballs for dinner. Her specialty from her grandmother in Sicily. Jared and Tony eat in silence.

"Cat got your tongues?" Aunt Agnes says.

Uncle Bruno doesn't say anything.

Uncle Bruno never says anything.

It's that kind of family.

Tony turns to me. "Jared and the guys and I are going to a movie tonight. You want to come?"

"Sure," I say surprised they want to spend any time with me.

They've been distant since I got here—nothing like the previous summers.

"Great!" Tony flashes me a smile.

Both he and Jared have grown into handsome young men. A lot different from the skinny kids I used to run through the fire hydrants with.

"We're going to see the new Black Widow movie," Jared adds. "We figured you'd like that. A strong woman, and all."

I simply nod. I've never considered myself a strong woman. Before now, I never considered myself a woman at all. I'm still in my teens.

Tony rises from the table and kisses Aunt Agnes's cheek. "Thanks for dinner, Ma." He nods to Bruno. "See you, Pop."

Uncle Bruno nods back, barely acknowledging his son. Some things never change.

Jared stands then. "You need to change or anything?" he asks me.

I look down at my shorts and tank top. "Yeah. I'll put on some jeans."

I hurry to the guest room and ditch my cutoffs for a pair of low-cut Calvins. The tank is a crop, so about three inches of my belly are on display.

I wonder if any of Jared and Tony's friends are cute? I haven't seen any of them for the last couple of years. Not since they were still playing stickball in the street or eating the hot dogs Aunt Agnes made for all the neighborhood kids at lunchtime.

A knock on the door. "Yeah, come in."

Jared enters. "You ready?"

"Yeah." I grab my purse and strap it across my body.

"Good. Let's go." Jared's voice cracks a little.

Weird. According to Aunt Agnes, his voice changed two summers ago. Why's it cracking?

I stop in the kitchen to say goodbye to Aunt Agnes.

"Have a good time, sweetie," she says.

Jared and I leave the brownstone.

"Where're Tony and the others?" I ask.

"They're waiting for us around the corner."

"Okay."

When I turn the corner, though, Tony isn't there.

No one is.

"Where is— No!"

Strong hands grab me, force me against a brick wall.

Then a prick in my neck.

Everything goes black as words make it to my ears.

Sorry, Katie. We need the money.

20

LUKE

I go to a meeting in the morning.

My name is Luke, and I'm an alcoholic.

My sponsor isn't here. He's in Phoenix, where I went through rehab. But I've met several people at this group who I can call if I feel like I'm ready to break.

"Welcome, everyone," Lynne, who runs the meetings, says. "It's a smaller group today, so there's time for everyone to talk. Who has something to share?"

"I almost took a drink last night," Barone says.

"But you didn't?"

"No."

"Good for you. You stayed strong. What happened?"

"I got a call from my ex..."

Barone drones on. Same old same old. Barone with her spiky blond hair and ripped clothing. Barone and her ex. She needs to move far away from that man.

Someone else starts speaking. Then another.

I'm wrapped in thoughts of Katelyn.

Until—

"Luke, you've been quiet this morning."

I jerk in my chair and look toward Lynne. "Have I?"

"Do you have anything to share?"

"I..." I clear my throat. "I met a woman."

They all perk up at that.

"And...?" Lynne prods.

"I'm taking it slow. Alcohol isn't my only addiction."

Snickers from the men in the group. And one woman.

"Slow is always good," Lynne says, "especially when you're grappling with staying sober. I'll be honest with you, Luke. It seems a little soon to me. We like to see people get a year into their sobriety before embarking on a relationship."

Lynne's words irk me slightly, but they're nothing new. I've heard her say the same to Barone and others, and in all honestly, I agree with her.

I clear my throat. "I know. I'm taking it slow."

"Are you still working at The Glass House?"

"Yeah."

"And serving drinks?"

"Yeah. It's tough sometimes, but I haven't fallen down the rabbit hole."

"Good for you."

"How do you do it?" Barone asks. "Every time I see a bottle of wine, it calls to me."

"It's not always easy," I admit. "I just remember everything I'll lose if I succumb."

No lie. These people don't even have a clue what I'm talking about. I can't tell them. I can't tell anyone.

"Yes," Lynne says. "We must stay strong. And Barone, congratulations! Today you get your six month chip."

Clapping hands echo throughout the small room.

Good on Barone. I've only been coming to this particular

group for two months, but I have to say, I'm proud of her. She struck me as a hot mess the first time I saw her, but the girl's determined. I'll give her that. She just needs to stay away from that loser ex of hers.

After the meeting, I'm noshing on my donut and bad coffee, when Barone approaches me.

"So you met a woman, huh?"

I swallow the bite of cruller. "Yeah."

"That's too bad." She twists her lips into a flirty pout.

Seriously? Barone is coming onto me? After she just told the tear-jerking story about running into her ex? How exactly am I supposed to reply?

"I was hoping"—she looks down at her lime green Chuck Taylors—"that maybe you might want to get some coffee. You know. Sometime."

I hold up my Styrofoam cup. "Like now, maybe?"

She blushes. "You know what I mean, Luke."

Yeah, she doesn't have to spell it out for me. Barone is a hot little number if you can get past the eyebrow ring and thrift store reject clothing. Too young for me. She's twenty-two. I know that because two weeks ago she announced it was her birthday, and how it feels so weird to be turning twenty-two and not celebrating with a drink.

I can only imagine what her twenty-first birthday must have been like.

"I'm at least ten years older than you are, Barone," I say.

"So? I'm legal and all."

And a hot mess in Chuckies.

"I'm not going to be anyone's rebound guy," I say. "You need to get over your ex first."

"Him? I'm totally over him."

"Right. That's why you almost fell off the wagon because of him."

She cocks her head and smiles. "Come on, Luke."

"You're a sweet kid—"

She winces at the word *kid*.—

"—but you and I aren't going to happen."

We were never going to happen anyway, but now that I've met Katelyn? *Never* takes on a new meaning.

She flounces off in a huff.

Yeah, that'll show me you're old enough to date me.

I resist rolling my eyes.

Lynne approaches me then. Now Lynne is a knockout—curve-a-licious figure and shiny chestnut hair—but I feel nothing. Not a damned thing. I haven't been attracted to a woman since I got out of rehab.

Not until Katelyn.

Lynne didn't come over to flirt, though. "Hey, Luke. Thanks for coming this morning. I hope it works out for you with the woman."

I swallow my bite of donut. "Strangely, I do too. I could have sworn I wasn't ready for this yet."

"I hear you. Sometimes when you meet the right person, things fall into place. Just remember to be careful. It's awfully soon for you."

Lynne moves on to the next person. She's a good group leader. She takes the time to talk to everyone personally after the meeting.

I guess that's why we all keep coming back.

Keep coming back. It works.

The mantra.

And the other mantra...

God, grant me the serenity to accept the things I cannot

change, the courage to change the things I can, and the wisdom to know the difference.

I try to live by that. I'm not big into religion or anything, so I'm praying more to my own consciousness than to any higher power.

But damn, there are things I can't change. I wish I could change big parts of my past, but they're already set in stone. The only thing I can change is the present, which I hope will lead to a better future. A future where I'm a good man—a man who's proud of who he is.

I believe I'll get there.

I have to believe it.

I finish my donut and trash the rest of the bad coffee. I'll stop at Starbucks and get a drinkable cup. I wave goodbye to Lynne and the others. Barone's back is turned. Just as well.

I mean nothing to her. The only reason she came onto me was because she knew I was interested in someone else. She's hung up on her ex, who seems like an asshole, but what do I know?

I head to the park for my jog.

And I try to accept the things I cannot change.

21

KATELYN

You don't have to do this, I tell myself. *You don't have to do it. You can turn back now. No one will ever know you were here.*

I go so far as to open my mouth to tell the cabbie to turn around, but the words don't materialize.

They stay in my head, chanting in a guttural chorus.

The drive through the Brooklyn streets takes me back. It's a chilly March day, but still some kids are out playing stickball.

For a moment, a smile curves my lips. How I loved those summers.

But my smile is short-lived.

The familiar brownstone looms in the distance. When the cabbie jerks to a stop, my heart nearly jumps out of my chest.

"Here you are, lady."

I slide my credit card and add a tip of fifteen percent. "Thanks."

"You want me to wait?"

Yes, please. Except I can't pay for wasted time. "No, thank you."

This is a pretty safe neighborhood. At least it was. My fate wasn't sealed because of a safety problem. No. It was sealed because my cousins got in with a bad crowd. I'm not sure why they did what they did, but I'm sure as hell going to find out.

I walk up the concrete steps to the door. The concrete is spalling, and grass and weeds grow through the cracks.

I consciously avoid the cracks. *Step on a crack, break your mother's back.* Funny. I've always avoided the cracks since I was a little kid, even when I was mad at my mom—which happened a lot. This time the act takes work, as the cracks are so numerous.

The door knocker. It's brass, with a wolf's head. I remember it. It always fascinated me. Brooklyn is so different from LA. East coast versus west coast. But so much more than that.

I inhale, touch the knocker, pause a moment, and then let it clank. Twice. And then a third time.

The peephole looms large in front of me, and I imagine eyes looking through it, assessing me.

The door opens, finally, and a young man stands there. "Yeah?"

"I'm looking for Agnes DeCarlo."

"She lives upstairs. I'll buzz her for you."

"Yeah. Okay. Thanks."

He holds the door open. "Come on in."

I follow him in. "Do you live here?"

"Yeah. Downstairs. I man the door to get a few bucks off my rent." He nods to a few chairs in the foyer. "Have a seat. I'll buzz Agnes for you. What's your name?"

"Katelyn Brooks. No. Wait. Tell her Katie Brooks."

Aunt Agnes always called me Katie. She was the only one. Except for Jared that one time.

"She says to go on up," the guy says a few minutes later.

I nod and follow the familiar staircase up to the second level of the brownstone. The door stands just as it did ten years ago. I knock.

The door opens. An old woman stands there. She's gray, her hair piled into a knot on the top of her head. She's gained weight, and her face now has wrinkles that divide her jowls like highways on a map.

But it's Agnes.

I clear my throat. "Hello...Aunt Agnes."

Her deep-set brown eyes nearly pop out of their sockets. "Katie? Little Katie?"

Little Katie? I was eighteen the last time she saw me.

"Yes."

"My God. We all thought..." She clasps her hand to her mouth. "But...you're here. Why didn't your mother call me? What happened? Where have you been?"

I could fill about ten volumes of books with the answers to her questions, and none of it is anything I want to talk about. But I came here for a reason—a reason that eludes me at the moment.

"Come in," Aunt Agnes says. "Please. Come right in."

I walk through the door. A golden retriever with a white mask around his pretty face sniffs at me.

"Go on, Rufus," Aunt Agnes says.

"He's okay. I don't mind." I pet his soft head.

"Old Roof is twelve years old, and he still gets up every time someone comes to the door. I wish I could say the same about your Uncle Bruno."

"Twelve years old?" I wrinkle my forehead. "Then I should remember him."

"No reason you should. We got him when he was four. One of Tony's friends was moving out of state and couldn't keep him."

"Oh." For some reason I feel better. For a moment I wondered if my memory had gone.

But no. I remember everything else about this place. The faux Turkish rug in the foyer, which now looks even more faded than it was. The mirror on the wall above the roll top desk. The scuffed hardwood. The living room, with the twin paintings of Jesus and Mary, and the green vinyl recliner, with Uncle Bruno still sitting in it as if he hasn't moved in ten years. Smoking his pipe, reading the paper, watching the TV, or snoozing. He gets up only to go to meals or go to the bathroom. Oh, and he farts. Even now the methane overpowers the pipe tobacco.

But it's the kitchen I remember most.

Is its retro décor still the same? Aqua blue and white? Does Aunt Agnes still call the refrigerator an icebox? Does she still keep canned goods in the coat closet in the hallway? I inhale. Yeah, the spicy scent of her marinara still drifts from the kitchen. Didn't matter what was on the stove. The kitchen always smelled like tomatoes, basil, and garlic.

"Sit down, Katie. Please." She nods toward the living room. "I'll get us a snack."

Instead I follow her to the kitchen and take a seat on one of the kitchen chairs. They've been reupholstered. They're a blue flower print now. Not the orange and green I remember.

But the chairs are the same. Retro design again, with chrome legs.

"I have some biscotti and oatmeal raisin cookies," Aunt Agnes says.

"No, thank you. I'm not hungry."

A few seconds later a plate appears in front of me anyway. I pick up a cookie and take a bite. Though I expect it to taste like sawdust, cinnamon and brown sugar explode across my tongue.

Aunt Agnes was always an amazing cook. I loved her meals, especially compared to my mother's Kraft macaroni and cheese and Hamburger Helper. More often it was fast food or takeout.

Macaroni and cheese. That was what Aunt Agnes truly did better than anyone. I couldn't stomach the Kraft stuff after tasting hers.

Aunt Agnes sits a glass of milk in front of me as well. I take a sip. Mmm. Whole milk, probably still delivered in glass bottles.

I feel like I've entered a time warp back to the 1950s.

"Katie." Aunt Agnes sits next to me. "Tell me. Tell me everything."

"I will," I say.

It's not a total lie. I'll tell her a few things. "But first, where are Tony and Jared?"

Aunt Agnes's face falls.

Bad news? Couldn't happen to two nicer guys. Though I feel for Aunt Agnes. She can't help it that her sons are derelicts.

"Oh, Katie." She shakes her head. "Tony's incarcerated at Atticus. And Jared..." Her eyes glaze over. "My Jared took his own life ten years ago."

"Ten years ago?" I gasp.

"Yes. I still can't fathom it. He was such a happy kid."

Ten years ago he was sixteen. I was eighteen. And he and Tony...

I reach forward and cover Aunt Agnes's hand with my own. "Tell me. Tell me what happened."

"For the life of me, I don't know. Bruno doesn't know. If Tony knows, he's not saying anything."

"Why is Tony in prison?" I ask.

"He got involved with some crack dealers or something. I don't know. He was eighteen when it all happened, so Bruno and I weren't involved. We tried to help him but he wouldn't take our help. All we know is he pleaded guilty to selling and possession of a controlled substance. He was supposed to get out on parole last year, but he got into a fight with another inmate, so they canceled his parole hearing."

"Drugs, huh?"

"Yes. For the love of God, I'm not sure how this happened. I thought I raised two good boys. Good Catholic boys. But—"

"Catholic?"

"Of course. You didn't know we were Catholic?"

"I did."

The crucifix in the hallway was a big clue. No, I'm just putting two and two together. A priest was involved in my capture. He was never there on the island, but he was involved.

"What parish do you go to, Aunt Agnes?"

"You know which parish, dear. You went with us to mass on occasion."

I did, but I don't remember. I was a kid, and kids find church of any sort boring as all get-out. "Yes, I'm sure I did. But I don't remember."

"It's a parish in Manhattan. St. Andrew's."

St. Andrew's. Doesn't ring a bell. Did Zee ever tell me

where that priest worked? I'm not actually sure, because I tried not to listen to anything other than her telling me someone new had been arrested. Whoever the priest was is probably either dead or behind bars now anyway.

I clear my throat. "I'm sorry about Jared."

"I know, Katie. I'll never get over it. He was my baby."

"Did he leave..." I clear my throat.

"A note? No. Nothing. Just shot himself in his bedroom upstairs. Where he got the gun I'll never know. The serial number was rubbed off."

So he was dealing in firearms. Or knew someone who was. His brother, perhaps?

Though they didn't pull a gun on me. They drugged me. I absently touch the side of my neck.

"I..." I clear my throat again and then take a drink of milk. It's creamy thickness coats my tongue. "I'd like to see Tony."

"They only let us visit on Thursdays."

"Okay. That's tomorrow."

"Bruno isn't going. He refuses to. But I'm going, of course. I'll never turn my back on my baby. Never in a million years."

"I'd like to go."

"You can come along, but I don't know if they'll let two of us in."

That doesn't matter. I don't want Agnes to be there when I talk to Tony.

"You know what?" I say. "I don't want to horn in on your visitation with your son."

"It's okay, sweetie. I'm sure he'd be glad to see you."

Actually, he probably won't. Testimony from me will put him away for another decade or more. But that's not why I want to talk to him. I need to find out how. And why. I just need some closure.

I take a bite of cookie, chew, swallow. "No, Aunt Agnes, but thank you for being willing to take me.

"If you're sure." Aunt Agnes doesn't push it. She probably doesn't want anyone horning in on her time with Tony either.

I don't blame her.

Do I tell her? Tell her what her beloved son did to me? Put me through?

Aunt Agnes was like a second mother to me. In fact, she showed me more affection than my own mother ever did.

I can't do that to her.

So much has been spoiled in my own life. I can't do it to someone else.

"I should be going," I say.

"Don't be silly. You came all this way." She cocks her head. "At least I assume you did. From LA?"

I shake my head. "I live in Manhattan now." By way of a South Pacific island where I was held captive for a freaking decade.

"You are? Then you must come on Sundays for supper. Please."

I'm never really hungry anymore, but Aunt Agnes's cookies sure tasted good. "Maybe I will."

"I insist. We'll expect you this Sunday at four. You remember, don't you?"

I nod. Sundays at Aunt Agnes's were always an early dinner at four p.m., and they were always an Italian feast.

I usually went home with a weight gain of at least five pounds after a week in Brooklyn. My mother hated that. She was convinced I was going to be some wafer-thin runway model.

Yeah, right.

"All right, I'll be here." I smile. "I need to go now." I punch in the number to call a cab.

"Where are you going? I can drive you. Mr. Luigi downstairs has an old Impala he lets me borrow sometimes."

"No, don't worry about that. I've already called for a cab."

"Uber's quicker."

"True, but..." I don't like the idea of getting into a car with a complete stranger. Of course, cabbies are strangers too.

God, I'm fucked in the head.

My text dings. "My cab will be here in about fifteen minutes."

"Good." Aunt Agnes smiles. "Then you have time for a few more cookies. Plus, I'll wrap some up for you to take home."

Before I can stop her, Aunt Agnes is back at the counter, hustling and bustling.

Uncle Bruno saunters into the kitchen then and meets my gaze.

"Hey, Uncle Bruno. Remember me? Katelyn?"

He grunts, nods, grabs a beer from the refrigerator, and heads back to the living room, taking a long drag of his pipe.

I pull out my phone. I hate to bother Zee when she just gave birth...

But I need a favor.

22

LUKE

I resist the urge to call Katelyn. I have to work, anyway. Lois shamefully flirts with me for the first two hours of my shift but then finally settles in her office to do paperwork by eight p.m. I'm on for another three hours.

I head to my next table—a threesome.

"Hello, I'm Luke and I'll be—" My mouth drops open.

Not just any threesome, but a Wolfe threesome. Rock Wolfe, his wife—a gorgeous blonde—and his brother Reid, husband to Zee. My old man knew their old man a lifetime ago. At least it seems like a lifetime ago.

And their old man? Makes my old man look like a fucking saint.

Hell, he even makes the old me look like a fucking saint.

What are the odds?

"...your server." I finally find my words. "Can I get you a cocktail?"

"Bourbon," Rock says.

"Any particular brand, Mr. Wolfe?"

"Whatever's closest to the bartender's reach is fine with me," he says.

I can't help a chuckle. "Good enough."

Reid scoffs. "Get the Pappy's, dumbass. You know you want to." Reid meets my gaze. "You have Pappy Van Winkle's?"

"Ten or fifteen year?" Nice. Pappy's is expensive, which means a nice tip.

"Fifteen, of course," Reid says, his eyes amused. "The ten is complete piss."

"Got it. For you, Mrs. Wolfe?"

Lacey Wolfe blushes. "Just water for me."

"My wife is expecting," Rock says.

"Oh! Congratulations. So your new daughter will have a cousin soon," I say to Reid.

"Yes. How do you know about my daughter?"

"I was your wife's waiter two nights ago when she went into labor."

Reid stands and holds out his hand. "Then I owe you my gratitude. Zee says you were very good to her friend."

"Katelyn? No problem."

"I understand you saw that she got home."

"It was no trouble at all, Mr. Wolfe."

"Reid, please. And Rock and Lacey." He gestures to his brother and sister-in-law.

"It's great to meet all of you. I'm Luke Johnson."

Reid pulls his wallet out of his pocket and extracts a business card. "If you ever need anything." He hands it to me. "Thank you again. Katelyn is very special to Zee."

"Thank you. I'll keep that I mind." I slide the card into my pocket. "Let me get those drinks started for you."

I amble to the bar and put in the order for the Pappy's

fifteen-year for Rock and Reid, all the while Reid's card is burning a hole in my pocket.

Man... I could get out of The Glass House. Away from serving alcohol.

I'm qualified to work at Wolfe Enterprises. I have an MBA in finance. Plus a lot of "business experience." Not the kind I'd put on a resume, but...

No.

Can't do it. Can't ask for a job. My only job is to stay under the radar, and already I'm known to four people in the Wolfe family—people who are the opposite of under the radar.

And then there's Katelyn.

Who is very special to Zee.

What is their connection?

I could call my father. He would know.

But then he'd know where I am. Unless I used a pay phone... If I could even find one. But he'd still know my vicinity.

No. Can't do it.

Luke Johnson is a waiter, a recovering alcoholic. Luke Johnson never went to college.

Luke Johnson is no one.

23

KATELYN

*C*all me anytime. Night or day.

Those were Zee's words. Tonight is merely forty-eight hours after she gave birth. Is she even home yet? Zee Wolfe no doubt gets the best post-natal care available. She may well still be in the hospital.

Call me anytime. Night or day.

I push send.

The phone rings. Then again. Three times. Four. Five. Si—

"Hello?"

Zee's voice. I freeze for a minute.

"Hello? Katelyn?"

Of course. My name shows up on her phone. God, I'm not thinking straight.

I clear my throat. "Zee, I'm sorry to bother you."

"You're no bother. Is everything okay?"

"I'm fine. But…"

"You wouldn't have called me if everything was fine. What is it? What can I do to help?"

Once again, Zee amazes me. She's been through so much, and she just brought another life into the world. Yet she's concerned with helping me.

"I'm actually fine. Truly. But I do need something."

"Of course. Anything that's within my power."

"There's a man in prison, upstate at Atticus, who I need to speak to. Anthony DeCarlo. He's my second cousin, and…"

"And…?"

"He's the reason I was taken. He and his brother drugged me with something, and the next thing I knew I was in that horrible place, running for my life in a concrete maze." I clear my throat again. "The place where we met. That first time."

"Oh… Can you talk to the brother?"

"No. He… He's dead."

"All right. I'll talk to Reid. We can probably get you on this guy's visitor list."

"I can go with his mother, my aunt, but she doesn't know anything about what happened to me and who was behind it. I can't do that to her. She already lost one son."

"Sounds like her kids got into some bad stuff."

"They did, obviously. But Aunt Agnes is the nicest person. How can apples fall so far from the tree?"

"I don't know, Katelyn, but it happens sometimes."

"I was only with them a week most summers. I don't know how they were raised the other fifty-one weeks." I spill out the whole story. Then, "I guess there was a lot of stuff I didn't see."

"Probably."

"Oh, there's one other thing," I say. "They're Catholic, and their parish is St. Andrew's."

Silence.

Silence so thick I can almost see it coming through the phone line in a fog.

Finally, "I think the parents are probably blameless in this situation," Zee says. "If they sent their kids to St. Andrew's."

I gulp audibly. "Oh?"

"The priest. Father Jim. He was the parish priest at St. Andrew's."

Another gulp. "He's the one who— Wait. *Was*?"

"He's dead. Didn't they tell you that at the retreat center?"

I search my mind. Did they? "They may have. The first few weeks at the center are kind of a blur."

"Totally understandable."

"Zee?"

"Yes?"

"How's the baby?"

"She's wonderful! She's sleeping in my arms right now."

"Are you still at the hospital?"

"Yes. They're springing us tomorrow."

"I'm sorry."

"For what?"

"I should have asked about her first thing. I've just... No. There's no excuse."

"Katelyn, it's okay. You have other things on your mind. You're totally forgiven. Besides, you named her."

I smile, even though Zee can't see me. I can't help it. "I can't take credit."

"Of course you can. Honor was your idea, and it's perfect. *She's* perfect."

"I can't wait to see her."

"She'll love her Auntie Katelyn."

Auntie Katelyn. Sweet.

"In fact... I promised Reid we'd talk to you together, but he'll forgive me. This is the perfect time."

"The perfect time for what?"

"To ask you to be Honor's godmother."

I nearly drop the phone but manage to increase my grip before it tumbles from my grasp. "I'm...honored." I can't help a chuckle. "But shouldn't you ask one of your sisters-in-law? Or a good friend?"

"I consider you a good friend, Katelyn. I... I owe you something."

"Zee, I owe you *everything*."

"No. Let me explain. I never forgave myself for leaving you. I should have helped you up. Gotten you out of there."

"I couldn't move, and you couldn't carry me. I'm just thankful you didn't do what I originally asked you to do."

"I couldn't have ended your life. But I never forgot you. And when I saw you that day on the island, sitting in the great room with *I Love Lucy* on the television... When you asked if we'd met... Katelyn, I felt like something had shifted in the world. I was so grateful that you were alive. That you *are* alive. You're an amazing woman, and just the kind of role model I want for my daughter."

Tears pool in my eyes. I sniffle. I should say something, but what? I'm totally unworthy of his honor.

Or am I?

I respect Zee so much, and if she feels I'm worthy...then maybe I *am* worthy.

"Thank you," I say quietly.

"Thank you," she says. "For my baby's name. For your strength. For your friendship."

I can't hold back then. I burst into tears.

"Katelyn..." Zee's voice in my ear, but I can't respond.

I'm too busy panting out sobs.

"Katelyn, honey, it's okay. Everything is okay."

"But you... I..." More racking sobs.

"Let me talk to Reid about this Anthony DeCarlo. Okay? I'm going to let you go, but I'm going to call you back in half an hour to check in. Okay?"

"Okay," I manage to gasp out.

I sob. I sob and sob and sob.

And for the first time in...forever?

I realize the sobs are not sad, but happy.

24

LUKE

My phone buzzes at eight a.m., just as I'm about to leave for a jog.

My heart skips. It's Katelyn!

"Hi, Katelyn," I say into the phone.

"Hi, Luke."

"To what do I owe this pleasure?"

"I was wondering...if you could do something for me."

"Of course. What do you need?"

"First of all, are you working tonight?"

"Yeah."

"What time?"

"I go in at five."

She pauses a moment. "Good. Could you take me somewhere around one o'clock?"

"Sure. Where?"

Another pause. Then, "Atticus Prison."

The phone slides out of my hand and hits the hardwood with a clatter. I hastily pick it up and glue it back to my ear.

"I'm going to need a little more information."

"I have to see my cousin. His name is Anthony. He's in prison there."

"Oh." Relief sweeps through me. A cousin. I can deal with that. "Of course."

"I got on his visitor's list, and I have to go at one because my aunt is going this morning. I don't want to disturb their time. But visitation is over at two, and I want at least an hour. I just need you to take me. They won't let us both go in. I just don't... I don't want to go alone."

"I understand." I wouldn't want to go to a prison alone either.

I came a hair's breadth away from a lifetime in one.

In fact, if anyone other than Katelyn were asking me to do this, the answer would be not only no, but hell no.

"I'll get a cab and come get you."

"You don't have a car?"

"No one has a car in New York, Katelyn."

"Oh. Yeah. Of course. But a cab's so expensive. It's upstate. About an hour away."

"I know where it is. Don't worry. It's on me."

"I couldn't."

"You didn't. I offered."

"I have money, Luke."

"So do I, and I can't think of anything better to spend it on than an afternoon with you." True words. Even a cab ride to a prison sounds good if Katelyn is involved.

"I'll be at your place around eleven. Sound good? Will that give us enough time?"

"Yeah. I think so. I'll eat an early lunch."

"Better yet, you and I will go to lunch beforehand. Name the place."

"I'm still new here. I don't know any places other than The Glass House and that Italian place we went to."

"Good enough. I'll walk to your place, we'll find a place for early lunch, and then we'll hail a cab and get to the prison."

"All right." I almost hear a smile in her voice. "Thank you, Luke."

"You're welcome. See you soon."

My day is suddenly better.

I'm going to see Katelyn today.

～

SHE'S WAITING for me on the sidewalk outside her building. Why doesn't she want me to go in and pick her up? I choose not to question this, though. I want to have a nice lunch with her.

Maybe find out why she's visiting her cousin in prison. Is it just a family visit? Or is there more to it?

I smile and brush my lips over her pink cheek. "Hi, Katelyn."

"Hi."

"There's a great little breakfast place a couple blocks over."

"Sounds good. I haven't had breakfast yet."

"They have amazing pancakes and waffles. Or you can have a sandwich. I think they start serving lunch around ten-thirty."

"Actually, pancakes sound good. My mom used to make pancakes. Out of a box, of course. She's a terrible cook. But the pancakes turned out perfect every time."

"Pancakes it is, then." I grab her hand.

She tenses for a moment but then I feel her relax. Her hand is kind of clammy, but so is mine. It's been a long time since I've been nervous around a woman. Definitely new to me.

Which is far from a bad thing.

We don't talk on the walk, but it feels very natural. Katelyn's not a big talker, which will make it all the more difficult for me to find out why exactly she's visiting her cousin in prison. She so was *not* an escort. Maybe it's none of my business. It probably isn't, though I can't help but feel that everything about Katelyn is my business.

No. Stop.

I won't go there. I won't treat Katelyn the way I treated the others. It's not fair to her. It's not fair to me, either. I won't sacrifice nearly a year's growth. I can't.

We're lucky to get a table as soon as we reach the café. A server takes our coffee orders—Katelyn likes hers black, same as I do. Not exactly a solid foundation for a relationship, but it's a start.

She buries her nose in the menu and widens her eyes.

"See something you like?"

"Blueberry cheesecake pancakes. That's got to be a thousand calories right there."

"You hardly need to worry about that."

She blushes—that rosy hue that I imagine going down past her V-neck to the swell of her breasts.

"I haven't been very hungry lately," she says.

"So? Order them, and only eat a couple bites if you want. There aren't any pancake police around." I smile.

That gets a giggle out of her.

Nice.

The sound of her voice brings me joy, especially when it's part of a laugh. I've never heard anything sweeter.

The server returns.

"The lady will have the blueberry cheesecake pancakes," I say, "and I'll have the short stack, butter and maple syrup."

"Very good." The server makes a notation and whisks away from the table.

"You're a purist," she says.

"I suppose so. When it comes to pancakes. And to black coffee."

"Do you have trouble staying away from alcohol?" she asks.

Hmm. That came out of nowhere. May as well be honest. "Sometimes. It's a daily battle."

"I don't know much about addiction," she says. "What do you know about drugs?"

I go rigid. Why is she asking me about drugs? Surely she can't know about *my* past.

Can she?

Before I can think of how to reply, she continues.

"This cousin I'm seeing today, Tony, he's in because of drug charges. Selling and possession."

"Oh." Relief sweeps through me like a desert breeze. "What kind of drugs?"

"I don't know. My aunt just said it was selling and possession of a controlled substance."

"Probably narcotics, then," I say a little too quickly.

"Narcotics?"

"Yeah. Oxycodone, Fentanyl, the like."

She cocks her head. "So you *do* know a thing or two about drugs."

"I've never taken them." No lie there. My drug was always alcohol, no matter what else I had access to.

And I had access to a lot.

"I was hoping it was something harmless, like pot."

"How long has he been inside?"

"Almost ten years."

"Then it wouldn't be pot. Hardly anyone gets incarcerated for pot anymore. It's legal in a lot of states, though still illegal at the federal level."

Damn. I should shut up. I wait. I wait for the inevitable question. *How do you know so much about drugs, Luke?*

But the question doesn't come.

"He was supposed to get out on parole last year," she continues, "but apparently he got into a fight or something and his hearing was canceled."

"Why do you want to see him?" I ask. "Are you close?"

She drops her gaze to the napkin in her lap.

"Katelyn?"

"We were once. When we were kids. But something happened to him."

I nod. I get it.

I've been there.

"What do you want to talk to him about?" I ask.

"I just want to...you know. To say hi."

Her gaze is still fixed on her lap.

Maybe she's telling the truth. Except if it *is* the truth, it's far from the whole truth. I hesitate to push her further, but my curiosity gets the better of me. I'm curious about all things Katelyn, including her jailbird cousin.

"When was the last time you saw him?"

"About ten years ago."

"I see." Though I don't see. I don't see at all.

"We weren't on the best of terms the last time we saw each other," she offers.

I resist the urge to lift my eyebrows. "Oh?"

She inhales sharply. "No. He... He did something to me. I need to ask him why he did it. What he had to gain. Was it worth it?"

I reach across the table and lay my hand over hers. "What, Katelyn? What did he do?"

25

KATELYN

I awaken in a dark room. I can't see. What happened? Am I blind? My heart races, and my fingers curl into fists.

Then my eyes adjust, and I exhale a sigh of heavy relief. I'm not blind.

I can see. But everything's dark. I'm on a bed. A twin bed with sheets and a dark comforter. Walls. Walls and a door. I get up, and—

"Oh!" My knees crumple beneath me, and I end up on the floor. It's cold.

Cold on my bare skin.

My clothes? Where are my clothes?

I reach for the bed and pull myself back onto it, sitting, my heart pounding like a jackhammer. I look around some more. A sink. A sink and a toilet. And...

The door.

I breathe in. Breathe out. I tell my legs to work, and...

I rise again.

This time I go slowly, still holding onto the side of the bed. Good.

I take a step. My head feels...strange. Kind of like it's in a fish bowl. I can almost see orange flecks of the goldfish swimming around. I know who I am, but I don't know where I am or how I got here.

Think, Katelyn, think.

I was home. Getting ready to fly to Newark to see Aunt Agnes and Uncle Bruno for the first time since...

No.

Wait.

I got there. I was in Brooklyn, in the brownstone.

Eating dinner with Aunt Agnes and Uncle Bruno. Uncle Bruno didn't talk. Uncle Bruno never talks. He just grunts.

I see it now. Tony and Jared were there, at the table.

We were...

We were going to go to a movie.

Right.

What movie did we see? I can't remember. Can't for the life of me re—

Then it comes to me, like a video playing in my mind. It's in color in my head, even though everything before my actual vision is in black and white because it's so dark in this room.

Sorry, Katie. We need the money.

We never got to the movie.

And I'm here.

My hands wander absently to my neck. I don't know why.

Until I touch a tender spot and wince.

My cousins. They...injected me with something.

I don't remember anything after that.

And now...

Now...

I'm here.

I'm here.

～

"WHAT, KATELYN?" Luke asks. "What did he do?"

I finally drag my gaze away from my lap and onto Luke.

He's so handsome. He's wearing long sleeves again, and I glance at the black and red on his left hand.

"What's that?" I ask.

"What's what?"

"Your tattoo."

"It's a...remnant of something I'd rather forget. I'm having it removed."

"Why?"

"Because it's a remnant of something I'd rather forget. Are you going to answer my question?"

Right. His question. What did he do? He being Tony.

I inhale and then let out a long sigh. I like this man. I have no reason to trust him, yet I feel I can. He's interested in me, but he's done nothing more than kiss me. He hasn't tried to get me into bed, and he hasn't bothered me unless I ask him to.

I've been dying to tell someone my troubles. Sure, I can talk to Macy, but that's in a purely professional setting. There's Zee, but she has a new baby, and I need to give her some space.

There's Lily, but she's been through the same thing or worse than I have. And Aspen, but if she's not coming to group, she's not up for any talking.

No. I need a neutral third party.

Maybe Luke can be that person.

I open my mouth, but the server arrives with our pancakes. I catch a whiff of the maple and butter of Luke's before the server sets down the blueberry mountain in front of me.

"Wow," I say, my eyes widening.

"Now that's a pancake palace," Luke says with a grin.

I inhale. Luke's butter and maple fades to black as the fruity and creamy scent of this blueberry extravaganza infuses my senses.

And for the first time since I got to Manhattan, I actually feel hungry.

I take a drink of coffee and then dig in. The flavors explode across my tongue, so perfectly blueberry. For a moment I feel like Violet Beauregarde from *Charlie and the Chocolate Factory*. Surely this will turn me blue, it's *so* blueberry.

"Good?" Luke asks.

All I can do is nod, my mouth is so full of berries and cream.

He grins and takes a bite of his own pancakes. "Purist or not, that looks like paradise on a plate."

I swallow. "It is."

"So..." He cuts another bite of pancake. "You going to tell me what's going on?"

Right. *What did he do*? That was the question.

I swallow my second bite of pancake. "My cousin, Tony DeCarlo—"

Luke stops his fork in midair. "DeCarlo? Anthony DeCarlo?"

"Yeah." I wrinkle my forehead. "I told you his name was Tony."

"Right, but you didn't mention his last name until now."

"So?"

"So...nothing."

"O...kay."

Weird. Does Luke know Tony? How could he? He said he grew up in LA, and Tony's never been out of Brooklyn—at least not that I know of—and he's been incarcerated for nearly ten years.

"So this Tony DeCarlo did something..." Luke begins.

"Yeah. We used to be close when we were kids, but I stopped going to Brooklyn once I hit high school, until the summer after I graduated. Aunt Agnes invited me out, and since I was going to begin college at Columbia in the fall anyway, I thought it would be nice to visit."

Luke nods, taking another bite of his pancakes. "You went to Columbia?"

I never got there, but that will only invite another question. I'm in, now. I'm going to tell him what happened. At least a little of what happened. I just won't tell him it took ten years of my life.

"I get there, to Brooklyn, and my cousins hardly give me the time of day. They were seventeen and sixteen at the time. I was eighteen. Anyway, after a day of ignoring me, they invite me to go to a movie with them one evening. I'm thrilled to have their attention, so I jump at the chance."

"What movie did you see?"

"I... I didn't see a movie."

"Oh?" He narrows his eyes.

"I honestly don't know what happened. I think someone injected me with something." My fingers trail to my neck—to that place they absently go when I recount this story.

Luke's cheeks redden. "Then what?" His tone is...different. Angry? Maybe.

"Then nothing. Until I woke up in a concrete room. It was

underground somewhere or it was built without any windows.

"Your cousin fucking drugged you and locked you up?"

"That's what I want to find out, Luke. That's why I have to see Tony. I never saw him or Jared again after that. I saw... other people."

"Who?"

How much do I divulge? The Wolfes kept the story out of the mainstream media for the women's sake, including me. Luke probably doesn't know anything. If I tell him, he'll walk away from me.

I can't risk that.

I need a friend now.

"Are you going to answer me?"

"I don't remember anything after that." The lie tastes bitter on my tongue.

"Katelyn..."

"Please. Don't."

He brushes his finger over my forearm. My hair stands on end. Just a minor touch sends a sizzle through me.

"You can trust me."

"Trust isn't the issue."

"Then what is it?"

Anthony DeCarlo.

It can't be. It just can't.

The Anthony DeCarlo I know is a prison informant somewhere in New York. I never knew where.

Anthony DeCarlo isn't an uncommon name, though, and Italian New Yorkers are a dime a dozen. It can't possibly be the same man.

I never knew why he was incarcerated in the first place. Didn't care. It ultimately didn't matter for my business.

Damn.

I hate thinking about my previous life.

It makes me face what a horrible human being I used to be.

One shot in the shoulder can change everything. Well—a gunshot and having no other choice.

"Katelyn..." I prod.

"I just need to see him. I need to know why."

"Why he drugged you and locked you in a room? Because he's a prick, Katelyn. A criminal and a prick."

A criminal and a prick.

Yeah. I know someone else who fits that description, and he's sitting at this table.

Can someone truly change?

I've stayed off the booze. I've been different with Katelyn than I ever was with any other woman I was involved with. I've stayed right in line with the law. Except for grabbing that asshole by the throat outside the restaurant, but he had it coming. I wish I'd smashed him into the brick. Fuck.

Katelyn shakes her head. "He's my cousin. I spent my summers with him for years. He taught me how to play stickball. He shared his baseball cards with me when he wouldn't let his brother or his friends anywhere near them. When we were seven and eight, we vowed to marry each other."

"You're cousins."

She laughs. "Second cousins. And we unmade the vow the next summer when we both had childhood crushes on schoolmates. But that's just how close we were. It made perfect sense at the time. We were kids, Luke."

I nod. I get it. They were close. Really close.

How could Anthony DeCarlo sell out his own cousin? His own cousin who was his close friend at one time?

People change.

Or people have no choice.

Having no choice can be the biggest game changer of all. I should know. In my case, it turned out to be a good thing. A lifesaver, even.

In DeCarlo's case, it seems to have led him down a path he can never retreat from.

It wasn't until he was in prison that he became an informant for my circles in LA.

Damn. He's done a lot worse than selling drugs and turning to narcing.

He harmed Katelyn.

"I'm going with you to see him," I say curtly.

"You can't," she says. "Reid only got my name on the visitor list."

Fuck. A year ago I could have walked into any prison and seen whoever I wanted.

Not anymore. That man no longer exists.

I inhale and hold it a few seconds. What now? I can't let Katelyn face the music alone.

"We'll tell them I'm your bodyguard," I say, thinking as I speak.

"What?"

"You heard me. This is a man who violated you. Injected you with a substance and then locked you in a room, Katelyn. There's every reason you might want a bodyguard with you."

"In a prison? Where there are guards everywhere?"

She's right. The bodyguard angle won't work. "Tell me, then. Tell me what happened."

She looks down, apparently very interested in her full plate of blueberry mush. For that's what it is now. I can't finish my own. My stomach feels like a bat is flying around inside it.

"Katelyn, please." If I don't find out, I think I might die. It's the weirdest feeling.

"That's it."

"That can't be it. How did you get out? What happened to you there?"

"I..."

"It's okay. You can trust me," I say again.

"The Wolfes..."

No.

Oh my God. No.

The pancakes in front of me no longer smell like melted butter and sweet syrup. They're disgusting. A glop of disgusting mess.

Life is a glop of disgusting mess.

This. This is how she knows the Wolfes.

"I owe the Wolfes everything," she says, "even though it was their father who kept me captive all those years."

I gulp, but I'm unable to move the giant lump that has formed in my throat. The aroma of breakfast is making me sick.

Except it's this knowledge that's making me sick. Derek Wolfe and his island. It's not common knowledge—somehow the media never got involved—but *I* know. I used to run in those circles.

Katelyn.

God, no. Not my Katelyn.

"Katelyn...baby..."

"I'm okay now. That's the main thing."

Okay? How can she be okay? What did they do to her? That derelict with the yellow eyes. My God, he was one of them. Why isn't he rotting in prison somewhere?

"It wasn't so bad. A lot of the women had it much worse than I did."

"Stop," I say, willing my voice to remain calm though I'm angry as hell and want to pull my hair out strand by strand. "Stop. Please."

I can't hear any more. I want to grab her. Haul her back to the table, kiss her senseless and tell her I'll never leave her side.

But my days of protecting women in that way are over.

She drops her mouth open. Then she stands abruptly and walks out of the restaurant.

I throw some bills on the table and follow her. She's pacing up and down the sidewalk. I resist the urge to grab her arm.

"Hey," I say. "It's okay. Everything's okay."

"I shouldn't have told you. You... You don't want to know me now, and I understand, I'll just—"

My God, is that what she thinks? "Katelyn, baby, no. I... None of this was your fault. I just can't... I can't... Damn!" I punch the brick wall.

It doesn't even hurt.

"Luke!" She stumbles backward, away from me.

I've scared her, which is the last thing I wanted.

I look down at my knuckles. They're covered in blood. Still no pain.

"I'm so sorry if I scared you. I just..."

She inches toward me. Meets my gaze. "I want to trust you. I need someone. I need someone who will just listen." She touches my hand that's still curled into a fist. "Does it hurt?"

"No." I may never feel pain again. Not until I rid the earth of every piece of shit that harmed this woman.

This isn't me. Not anymore. This can't be me.

I can't protect her.

"Luke..."

I exhale slowly. "I can be that person. I know we just met, Katelyn, but I like you. I like you a lot." The word love hovers on my tongue, but neither of us is ready to go there yet.

But it's just around the corner. Already I feel it. This need. This meeting of souls. Am I ready for it? Hell, no. But it's here, and I have to deal with it.

I take her hand, and together we walk slowly, getting growls from people behind us who have to pass us.

I don't care.

I don't care about anything except Katelyn in this moment.

"Ten years," she says finally.

I'm going to lose my pancakes now. Really lose them, right here on the sidewalk. Because I know. I already know.

My old man knew about Derek Wolfe's island in the South Pacific, where the richest of the rich went to hunt. I always assumed they were hunting something exotic—animals they brought in illegally from Africa.

Only recently did I find out the truth. I only hope she doesn't ask me how I know. I'm not sure I have the heart to lie to her. Not about this.

"Baby, oh my God." I cup her cheek.

She turns her face into my palm. Her lips brush my skin.

"I'm so sorry," I say. "And your own cousin sold you into it?"

"I believe he must have. Both of them, actually. And Jared couldn't deal with what he did so he committed suicide. And Tony..."

"Tony got in even deeper, it sounds like." She has no idea how deep, if indeed he's the Anthony DeCarlo I think he is.

"I have to know," she says. "That's why I have to see Tony. I have to know why he'd do that to me."

"Oh, baby. There's only one reason a man does that kind of shit. For the money. He needed the money."

"But he was a good man," she says. "He's my cousin."

"Your cousin who's doing time for drug charges. My guess is he got into debt with some kingpin or loan shark and it was either you or him."

"You mean they'd kill him?"

"Hell, no. A dead man can't pay his debts. They'd break a couple legs, scare him enough so he'd find a way to pay."

"I guess he found a way without getting his legs broken, then." She sniffles.

"I'll fucking kill him." Already my hands are in fists again, and the burning in my bloody knuckles only spurs me on.

"No, please. You can't get to him anyway. Please. He's not you. I couldn't bear it if you became someone like him. Please, Luke. You're everything that's good in this world."

Everything that's good in this world.

If only she knew.

But she doesn't. She sees only what is now. This woman believes in me. Believes in what I can be.

And for the first time, I begin to believe in myself.

I'm more than my past.

I'll prove it to Katelyn. I'll prove it to everyone.

I'll prove it to myself.

27

KATELYN

A guard stands behind me as I sit at the Formica desk. An old-fashioned phone is attached to the wall. It reminds me of study carrels. The kind I never got to use because I never went to college.

Columbia was ripped from me the day Tony drugged me.

My vision is blurred when a man, his hands chained, is escorted to the other side of the plexiglass. He's not wearing prison orange or blues. It's a dirty beige color, looks like surgical scrubs.

I force myself to meet his gaze, but my vision is still blurred.

I don't know why. I'm not crying. I can't cry. It's like my tear ducts have gone on hiatus. My vocal cords and optic nerves have as well, apparently.

The man picks up the phone on his side.

I do the same.

"What do you want?" a voice says in my ear.

Is it Tony's voice? It's been so long. I think it might be, but it sounds different. It's a little hoarse, but it's deep.

Finally my vision is restored. I take in the face on the other side of the glass. Dark brown hair shaved close to his head. Dark brown eyes and bushy brows that could use a good plucking.

Just like Uncle Bruno's.

Except Tony was handsome. Really handsome. A young Marlon Brando lookalike.

Not this Tony. This Tony has graying stubble and a scar across his left cheek. His lips are full but chapped. Looking closely, I see the flaky dried skin on them.

I clear my throat and hope my vocal cords are back online. "Hello, Tony."

"Who are you?" He narrows his eyes. "Fuck, no. Not Katelyn."

I nod. "It's me."

He nearly drops the phone. "Fuck," he says again.

"I have a question for you," I say.

"What?" he spits out.

"Why? Why did you do what you did?"

He doesn't answer right away. I fear he may not, when finally—

"I didn't want to."

"That's not an answer."

"I had no choice."

"Bull. There's always a choice."

"I was selfish," he says. "It was you or me."

I don't know why I'm surprised, but I am. I was holding out a tiny sliver of hope that somewhere inside this man was the Tony who shared his shaved ice with me. The Tony who cheered me on at stickball even though I sucked at it. The Tony who once vowed to marry me when he was seven and I was eight.

Apparently not.

"You got into trouble."

"Well, duh. I'm in prison, for God's sake."

"You weren't in prison then."

"Look, I've done my penance for that. It cost me my brother."

"It cost you your cousin, too."

He looks down. Is that remorse I see in his eyes?

I can't tell through the plexiglass. It's not exactly clean. Plus...he looks so different from what I remember. He looks tired. Fatigued. Used up.

I can relate.

"You're still here," he finally says.

"No thanks to you. I was rescued by some heroic and honorable people."

"Good on them."

"Cut the crap, Tony." Courage courses through me. A welcome emotion. "Why? Why did it have to be me?"

"Would you rather it have been someone else?"

"Don't put me on the defensive. I'm not the one who screwed up. I'm not the one behind bars because of my screwups."

"Low blow."

"Low blow? Really? You had me drugged, kidnapped, raped, hunted, and you're telling me I dealt a low blow?"

He nearly drops the phone receiver. "What? *Hunted*?"

"You didn't know where you sent me? Give me a break."

"Raped? Hunted? Hell no, Katelyn. Father Jim said you'd be a nanny for some rich people."

My jaw drops.

Until I regain my composure. For a split second, I almost believed him.

"That's crap," I say.

"It's not crap. I swear to you. He said he had some rich parishioners who needed a nanny and they didn't want an undocumented person. They wanted a nice girl. He said you'd be taken care of, not harmed."

"He lied," I say point blank. "He fucking lied to you, Tony. Or you're lying to me, because I don't for a minute think you were gullible enough to believe that horseshit."

"He's a priest. Of course I believed him."

"And you think it's just normal for priests to advocate drugging women and forcing them into servitude? That works for you?"

"No, I—"

"You needed money Why?"

"I...owed some dangerous people."

"You were seventeen years old, for God's sake. Who the hell could you possibly owe?"

"You don't want to know."

"That's where you're wrong. I *do* want to know. That's why I'm here. I need to know what was so important that you had to sacrifice me. Your cousin."

"Second cousin," he scoffs.

"You think that makes a difference?"

"What do you want from me, Katelyn? An apology? What the fuck would that do?"

Do I want an apology? No. An apology won't erase what happened.

And then I have an epiphany. Knowing why won't erase what happened either.

I hang up the phone. "Goodbye, Tony."

I know he can't hear me through the plexiglass. I don't care.

"I'm done here," I tell the guard.

I jolt as something crashes against the plexiglass. It's Tony, knocking his bound hands against it. A guard grabs him by the shoulders and drags him away.

"I'm not sure your friend is as done as you are," the guard says to me.

"He's not my friend."

"Oh? Then why did you want to see him?"

"He's my cousin. Second cousin. I thought I wanted some answers, but it turns out I don't."

The guard says nothing, just leads me out, back to the area where Luke is waiting for me.

He doesn't look happy.

28

LUKE

I made a phone call while I was waiting. To an old contact at the FBI—one of the only two people who know where I am. He wasn't thrilled with my request, but when I told him the details, he said he'd make it happen.

I'll be back here tomorrow, same time, without Katelyn.

And I'll be talking to Anthony DeCarlo.

Katelyn has a smile on her face, which surprises me more than a little. I rise when the guard leads her into the waiting area.

"Hey," I say. "How'd it go?"

"Okay." She nods, still smiling. Sort of.

"Just okay?"

"Yeah. I was looking for... Honestly, I'm not sure what I was looking for. Maybe some closure, but I realized something."

"What's that?"

"Nothing he could possibly say would change anything. And nothing he could possibly say would make me understand why he forsook me the way he did."

"You're probably right." I wince. My hand is starting to throb now.

"So I'm done here. He didn't apologize, and it doesn't matter. It is what it is."

"It doesn't have to be."

"But it is, Luke. Nothing can change the past, and nothing can make me feel better about it. My cousin—who I once loved—isn't the person he was when we were young."

"He was a child then."

"Right. But he was a good child. He's not a good man."

He's not a good man.

Her words spear into my heart, and the pain in my knuckles doubles, as hundreds of knives are slicing into me.

For most of my adult life, I wasn't a good man, either.

I've made a commitment to change. Getting off the sauce was a good start, but I have so much farther to go. I want to get there, and now that I've met Katelyn, I want it even more.

I was as addicted to women as I was to alcohol. But the difference is that I can't stay off women forever.

I don't want to.

I want to be the man I know I can be with some help.

And Katelyn makes me want that even more.

She's been through hell, and I want to help her see that life can be good. Life can be happy.

And while I show her, I'll show myself.

"He'll never be the kind of man you are, Luke."

Wow. Such words. She has no idea what they mean to me. I could easily be behind bars as well, with no freaking chance for parole.

I got lucky. Damned lucky, and I'm not going to waste the chance.

Which means I probably shouldn't come back here tomorrow to see Anthony DeCarlo.

I'll sleep on it.

Except I already know I'm coming back. Katelyn is that important to me, and I'm going to find out exactly what the hell he did to her.

And why.

"Let's get home," I say to Katelyn.

"What time do you have to be at work?"

I check my phone. "I've got a few hours yet."

"Could we..."

"Could we what?"

"Could we go to your place?"

My heart nearly stops. Is she asking for sex? Because I'm not sure she's ready.

I'm not sure I'm ready.

Though my cock has other ideas. It's already tightening to the point of discomfort inside my jeans.

"Are you sure?"

"Yeah. I'm sure. I'm not saying I want to...you know."

"That's okay. What do you want, Katelyn?"

"First, I want to clean you up. Bandage your knuckles. Maybe give you some ibuprofen. Then I want to be with you. I want you to hold me. I want you to remind me that good men still exist in the world."

I'm about ready to melt into a puddle. God, she gets to me. She makes me want to be a better man.

The best man.

No woman ever made me want that before.

Sure, I'm off the booze and I've been through some therapy, but the core of a person doesn't change. Just their environment. Their attitude.

For Katelyn, I will be a better man.

~

"IT'S SMALL," she says of my studio.

"It's cozy," I return.

She smiles. "It is. I like it." She walks around the room and stops next to my bed.

Trepidation exudes from her pores. The old me would be using my tried-and-true seduction methods and have her screaming between the sheets in ten minutes.

It's tempting...

She makes me want to be a better man.

It's still tempting.

But I won't succumb. I've come too far, and I care too much about her wellbeing.

"Let's take care of your hand," she says.

I walk toward her slowly, touch her soft cheek. "I've got it."

I head into my bathroom, wash the wound, and do the best I can with antibacterial ointment and a few small bandages.

A moment later, I'm next to Katelyn, who's still next to the bed. I touch her cheek again. "Tell me what you want. Anything. It's yours."

"You can't give me what I ultimately want."

"I can try."

She sighs. "You can't erase my past."

"You can't erase mine either," I say, "but together we can make a better future."

She sighs then—a soft moan that echoes through my small abode and into my very soul.

I push a lock of her blond hair out of her eyes and gaze into them.

So blue, like the sky right at noon, only the sun isn't shining in her today. She's troubled.

And I understand.

I wish I could erase her past. I'd do it in a minute, even if it meant giving my own life. The idea frightens me, and what frightens me more is that I mean it with all my heart. I can't erase her past, but I can hold her. That's what she asked for at the prison.

I close the small distance between us and take her in my arms. She melts against me, so perfectly fitted, as if she were made for me. Will it feel this way when we make love? Will I enter her and feel as though she were molded specifically for me?

Already I know the answer is yes.

She will.

She already is.

So I can wait.

I can wait until she's ready. And if she's never ready?

This will be enough.

Katelyn, in my arms, her sweet fragrance tingling in my nose, will be enough.

I kiss the top of her head, inhale the minty scent of her shampoo. Or is it even her shampoo? Perhaps she just smells that sweet. Minty and fragrant. Supple and divine.

She pulls away then, and I have to hold back a whimper at the loss of her body against mine. She sits on my bed and pats the spot next to her.

She's not asking for sex. I only wish she were, but in my heart of hearts, I know I'm no more ready than she is for that step.

I can wait.

Forever if I must.

That's how important this woman has become to me in the last few days.

I feel something different than I've ever felt.

Is it love?

I've been quick to fall in love before, but I know now that I was never in love. I was in love with controlling women. Making them slaves to my desires and needs.

I won't do that to Katelyn.

She's been a slave long enough.

Never again will she be bound to serve another man. I'll make sure of it.

She leans against me and then slowly falls backward and scoots sideways until she's lying down, her head on one of my pillows. I crawl next to her and wrap her into my arms.

I lie with her, body to body, separated only by our garments.

I breathe in her fragrance, her very essence.

And I know.

I'll do anything for her.

Fucking anything.

29

KATELYN

He doesn't try anything.
And I find that I'm...
Disappointed.

I want him. I want him so badly, and I never imagined wanting a man again, not after what I've been through at men's hands.

He holds me tight against him, and he's not unaffected. I feel his hardness pressing against me—that part of his body common to all other men, including those who violated me relentlessly for so long.

All except for Ice Man. He never went there, but he was still my worst nightmare on that island.

"What if we went away?" Luke whispers. "I can get a few days off. We can escape somewhere. Somewhere tropical."

I go rigid.

Tropical is the last place I want.

He jerks away slightly. "God, Katelyn. I'm sorry."

"It's okay."

"It's not okay. I wasn't thinking. Tropical won't work at all.

What about upstate? To the mountains? Or Lake Placid? We could take a few days and—"

I stop him with two fingers against his full lips. "This is all I need, Luke. To be right here, in your arms."

He pulls me back toward him. "That I can definitely do."

Kiss me.

Kiss me.

Kiss me.

I want to say the words so badly. It's not like we've never kissed before. But kissing leads to...other things. Things I want desperately but know I can't have. Not yet.

I never even imagined I'd want them again.

We've kissed before, but it was in the alley behind The Glass House. It couldn't go any farther back there.

Here, though? It could go all the way, and as much as the idea appeals to me, I can't.

He pulls back a little then and plays with a strand of my hair. "You're so beautiful."

"So are you," I say on a sigh.

He smiles. "No one's ever called me beautiful before."

"You are, though. Your hair. It's so black. Like night."

He tenses slightly. Did I say something wrong?

"Would you take off your shirt?" I ask.

"What for?"

"I want to see the rest of your tattoo."

Tension rises in him again. I can almost see it floating off him in dark waves. "That tattoo no longer has any meaning for me."

"I understand. I still want to see it. Tattoos are so sexy on men."

Funny that I still feel that way, but the men on the island rarely had tattoos, and if they did, they were small and insignificant. Treasure Island catered to the rich and famous —the people who had to look good for the cameras and be professional and respectful in their actual lives. They came to the island to act out their darkest fantasies and fetishes.

They could be their true selves there.

And their true selves were vicious and psychotic.

"I wear long sleeves for a reason, Katelyn."

"I know."

"So you understand, then, why I don't want to show you the tattoo."

"I suppose." I trail a finger over his stubbled cheek. "Please?"

It's a dirty trick. He likes me, and I think maybe I can get away with it. He sighs and sits up. Then he begins to unbutton his shirt.

And I feel like a heel.

I pull myself up next to him and place my hand over his to stop his unbuttoning. "It's okay. Don't. I shouldn't have been so persistent."

"I want to please you, Katelyn."

"Then kiss me, Luke. Please."

His lips are on mine then, and it's far from the gentle kisses we've shared before. This kiss is raw and untamed, and I part my lips eagerly to invite him in.

I melt against him, letting him take my lips, my mouth, my tongue, and I revel in it. Revel in the rawness yet pureness of it.

I've never been kissed like this before, and though I should be fearful, I'm not. This is Luke. Luke, who's kind and gentle, who would never hurt me.

We kiss for several moments, and the nearly visible passion between us only grows.

I feel that tickle between my legs—that beautiful feeling that I feared might be gone forever.

It's there.

And it wants more.

I tangle my fingers in his dark hair, run them over the outer shell of his ear, finger the small diamond stud in his lobe.

He groans—a humming growl that vibrates through our bodies and outward, taking over the small room.

All I hear is his groan, and all I feel are our tongues tangling together. All I see before my closed eyes is the lust that lies thick in the room. And all I smell is Luke. Luke and the outdoors and the masculine scent of coffee and leather.

I cup both his cheeks then, deepening the kiss. I never want it to end. Sure, Luke has to go to work in an hour, but we can kiss until then.

An hour of kissing Luke... Would anything be better than that?

I jolt.

Luke's hand. It's on my breast.

And I don't hate it.

I like it, in fact, and my nipple hardens. I ache for his fingers, his lips, his teeth on my nipples. All over my body.

I even want...

I want that part of him. That most intimate part of him inside the most intimate part of me.

He breaks the kiss. "Okay?"

"Yes. Okay."

He fingers my nipple through my clothes. And oh my God, I think I may burst into flames for wanting him so much.

"Please..." I rasp.

"What?"

"Please... I don't know. I want... I want..."

"What? What do you want, Katelyn?"

"I want...you. I want what I can't have."

"You can have it," he says, "but are you sure?"

"No, Luke, I'm not sure of anything anymore, except that I want you right now. At this very moment. Will I regret it later? Maybe. Am I ready for it? No. But that doesn't change what I feel. What my body yearns for. I want you. Inside me, Luke. I want you to fuck me."

Even *I* am shocked at my words. I said fuck? Not make love?

"I won't fuck you, Katelyn," he says.

Loss travels through me at top speed. I bite my lip. He's right, of course. It's not what I need. It's not—

"I will, though, make love to you."

"Oh God, please, Luke."

"But not right now."

I jerk away from him, stare into his eyes.

"What?" I grit out.

"I have to be at work in thirty minutes. I'm not going to do a *wham, bam, thank you, ma'am*. You deserve better than that."

"But I want—"

"You deserve better than that, Katelyn, and frankly, so do I."

I place my hand on the bulge in his jeans. "Are you sure about that?"

"Fuck," he says through gritted teeth. "What do you want me to say? That I'll fuck you silly? I could, you know. I want you so badly that I ache to the very bottoms of my feet. My whole body wants you. Needs you. But you've been through so much, and I won't take advantage of that."

"Luke..."

"Stop it. Stop it now. Don't think this is easy for me. You're basically giving me permission to ram my cock into you and fuck you silly, and trust me when I say I want it as much—probably more—than you do right now. But I'm trying to be a man here."

"A man would—"

"A man would *not*," he says. "A man who cares about a woman would not." He rolls away from me, sits up, and leaves the bed.

Is he angry? "Luke?"

"I need a minute." He walks toward a closed door, opens it, and enters, closing it once more.

The bathroom, probably.

I don't want to think about what he's doing in there. Then I know when I hear the whoosh of the shower. I hear everything. This place is so small, I can hear everything that goes on in the bathroom.

A cold shower.

I've driven him to this.

I'm not being fair to him.

Because he's ultimately right.

I'm not ready. Maybe for lovemaking with a partner who takes it slow and steady. But for a quick fuck?

I'm not ready for that, and it would probably leave me feeling empty. I don't want to feel empty. I'm tired of feeling empty.

A few minutes later, Luke comes out of the bathroom wrapped in a towel. I stop myself from getting up and making him turn toward me so I can see the tattoo.

He denied me out of respect, and I have to do the same

for him. He's not ready to show me the tattoo for whatever reason, and I must respect that.

He pulls underwear out of a short chest of drawers and a clean white shirt out of his closet. He puts them on, and only then, when his arm is covered, does he turn to me. "I have to go to work. You're welcome to stay here, Katelyn. You're safe here, and I'll be back around midnight. There's food in the fridge if you get hungry, or there's a pile of takeout menus on the counter. The Thai place is really good, and they deliver quickly because they're so close."

I bite my lip.

He puts on a pair of black pants and then socks and shoes. His work attire. Then he comes back to the bed and sits down, pushing my hair out of my face once more.

"You make it hard to be a good man," he says. "But you also make it extremely easy."

"What does that mean?"

He smiles, cups my cheek. Brushes his lips softly over mine. "It means I want you so much I can't see straight. I was a hair's breadth away from giving you the quick fuck of the century. But it also means you make me want to be better than that. I want to be the best man I can be for you, and that means saying no when it's the best thing for someone I care about."

My mouth drops open.

He trails his finger over my bottom lip. "Freaked you out, huh?"

"No. Not at all." I kiss the tip of his finger. "I just can't believe a man like you exists in this city. Heck, on this planet."

"I wasn't always this good," he says, "but you make me want to be."

"You're amazing, Luke."

"*You* are." He kisses me again. "Stay as long as you'd like. The only thing I ask is that if you leave, please text me when you're safely back at your place." One more kiss. "But I hope you'll stay. I can't think of anything more wonderful than coming home to you tonight."

30

LUKE

The cold shower didn't do much for me. Katelyn invades my thoughts, until—

I see my first table on my shift.

It's that man. Pollack. From the other night. The man who kept bothering Katelyn.

For a split second, I think about trading tables with Travis, but then I change my mind. Keep your enemies closer and all.

And anyone who affects Katelyn negatively is definitely my enemy.

I stride confidently—or so I hope—toward the table. There was a time in the not-so-distant past where nothing frightened me. I had the confidence of a seasoned criminal.

Which makes sense, of course.

I'm still me, but I'm aware of my limitations now. My shoulder wound aches. It always aches when I think about who I used to be. It's my reminder never to go there again.

I'm not frightened of Pollack. I can pummel him in my sleep.

But I'm no longer the same person I was—the person who used money and brawn to get what he wanted at all costs.

I wasn't a good man then.

I want to be a good man now. For Katelyn. And for myself.

I approach the table. Pollack sits with another guy. Both of them are dressed in designer suits. Businessmen. Rich businessmen.

My knuckles whiten around the short yellow pencil I'm holding, and—

Snap!

It cracks into two pieces.

I inhale, hold it, exhale.

No. I will not ask Travis to trade tables.

Lois brushes past me then. "Luke?"

"Yes?" I say more sharply than I mean to.

"Everything okay?"

"Yes. Why do you ask?" My God, I sound like a robot.

"You look...a little tense."

"I'm fine. I need to get a new pencil." I whisk past her, grab what I need, and head back to Pollack's table.

"Good evening," I say without smiling. "I'm Luke, and I'll be your server this evening. Would you like to begin with a cocktail?"

Pollack turns toward me. Looks me up and down. Then, "Yes, thank you. I'll have a Sapphire and tonic. How about you, Glen?"

Glen, presumably, meets my gaze. "Same. Thanks."

I scribble their orders on my pad with my brand new sharpened pencil...while I think about plunging the graphite point into Pollack's neck.

So this is how it will be. I wait on this bastard, and he pretends like everything's okay.

Fine. Two can play that game. I just have to figure out how to get the information I need on the sly.

I head to the bar and put in the order. Each time gets slightly easier, but still, the alcohol calls to me. I will never heed that call. Especially now that I've met Katelyn. She deserves me whole.

I take two more drink orders and then turn them in, at the same time picking up Pollack's and his guest's. I walk them slowly back to the table. The temptation to "accidently" pour the gin and tonic down the front of his silk designer neckwear is pretty great.

I breathe in again. "Here you are. Two Sapphire and tonics." I place a drink in front of each of them. "Would you care to order appetizers?"

"What are the specials tonight?" Glen asks.

An idea spears into my head. "We have a wonderful swordfish from the South Pacific."

Pollack goes rigid.

Yup. Just as I thought. He was there. This derelict hunted and raped my Katelyn.

I scan Glen's face. He seems unaffected. Good for him. I only have one derelict to deal with this evening.

"How is the swordfish cooked?" Glen asks.

"It's grilled, with a guava and mango salsa on the side. Served with fresh broccoli and asparagus spears."

"That sounds amazing," Glen says, closing his menu. "Put me down for that."

"So no appetizers, then?" I say.

"Not for me," Glen replies.

"And you"—I clear my throat of the nausea—"sir?"

Pollack stares at his menu, his hand trembling slightly. Good. I've got him on edge. He knows I know. What an idiot. He should have known better than to approach Katelyn. He's damned lucky he's not rotting in prison for what he did. How did he get off?

"Sir?" I say again, this time very aware of my clenched jaw.

He closes his menu. "Just a salad with ranch dressing, please. I've lost my appetite."

I hold back a scoff. "I'll get these orders in right away. Enjoy your cocktails."

I take the order to the kitchen and then head straight to the men's room.

I need a fucking breather.

31

KATELYN

I should go back to my place. Though Luke's small studio feels like home more than my own apartment does. I've been at my place for less than a week, so of course it doesn't feel like home yet. That makes perfect sense. What doesn't make sense is that Luke's place feels very much like home.

I've been lying here for a few hours, falling in and out of an alpha dream state. Not asleep, but in that lovely place between the awake and asleep world. A place I often escaped to on the island, when I had free time. Free time didn't come often, but when it did, I made it count.

Perhaps that's why I was able to leave the center before a lot of the other women. I escaped when I could, even if it was only in my head.

That was part of how I found my strength.

I rise from Luke's bed and pad to the bathroom. I inhale the scent of the piney soap from his shower before he left for work. I use the toilet quickly and then look around for the hand soap. The tiny bathroom is so small and there's no counter space, so I open the mirrored cabinet above the sink. Sure enough, there's a bottle of hand soap right next to some contact lens solution and a case. Hmm. He wears contacts. Not unusual.

I grab the hand soap, when my gaze falls on something that *is* unusual.

I quickly wash my hands and replace the hand soap and then grab the bottle of what appears to be hair color. Not hair color off the drugstore shelf, either. This is that expensive stuff you order online. The color is called raven 10—darkest brown black.

Except this online place mixes color for each individual, which means Luke had this mixed for him.

Maybe he's simply going gray, and he wants to look younger.

Except most men look amazing with a little gray. Women, on the other hand, just look old. One of life's many unfairnesses.

Don't dwell on it, Katelyn. It's not your business, anyway.

True story. But he told me to stay. Surely he'd know I'd eventually have to use the bathroom and wash my hands, so it's not like he thought I wouldn't see the hair color.

I'm reading way too much into this. Way, way too much. He invited me to stay here, so stay I will. Curiosity wells in me. This place is tiny. I could easily riffle through everything before Luke gets home at eleven.

That's not me, though. I'll curb the curiosity. I don't want to lose Luke's trust. I'll simply ask him about the hair color when he comes home. I found it innocently enough. The explanation is most likely equally innocent. He likes the color. Or he's covering gray.

Except I'm not convincing myself of anything.

I've grown cynical because of my time in captivity. I've learned to never accept things at face value.

I need to get over that.

So I won't ask about the hair color. And I'll stop asking about the tattoo. Neither is my business.

I leave the bathroom and head toward the kitchenette where Luke left the takeout menus. First things first. I'll check the fridge. I open it, and inside is a loaf of wheat bread and some deli meats. Perfect. A turkey sandwich will work just fine. No seafood in the fridge. Good.

I pull out the ingredients and assemble a sandwich quickly. I grab a can of sparkling water as well and sit at the tiny table next to the kitchenette. A few magazines sit there. *Newsweek* and *Esquire*. No surprise there.

I thumb through *Newsweek*. I'm determined to keep apprised of what's going on in the world since I spent the better part of the last decade knowing nothing. We had a TV in the common room, but all it played were old sitcoms from the fifties and sixties. I know all the episodes of *I Love Lucy* by heart.

When all that is left of my sandwich is a few crumbs, I wash the plate.

Is Luke's hair not naturally black? It's so dark, but it doesn't look fake. It's not blue black or pure black.

I reach to place the plate inside the cupboard where I found it, when a memory jars me. I grab the counter.

∾

A PLATE.

A plate sits on the table in the common room. I've never seen it before. We're not allowed to have anything porcelain that can break into anything with sharp edges.

Anything that could be a weapon.

I examine it more closely. It's definitely glass or porcelain. Not plastic or melamine, even, which we're still not allowed to have.

We eat off all paper products with food that can be hand held. We're not even allowed to have plastic flatware that can be made into a shiv.

Yeah, they've thought of everything.

So why is this plate here?

I look around. A guard lounges at the front desk, but he's not looking my way.

I grab the plate quickly and hide it under my shirt, and then I make my way to my dorm room.

I share a room with Emerald. She has green eyes, which is I assume how she got her name, but who really knows? Who really cares? I don't know her real name. We're forbidden to use our real names.

I know what mine is, though.

Katelyn. My name is Katelyn. I'm determined I'll never forget it.

Now, the plate... Should I break it now? Make a weapon?

No. Someone might hear the crash.

Under my mattress. Between the mattress and box springs. Except it's not box springs so much as it is just a piece of plywood. We change our own sheets. They appear once a week, and we leave the dirties outside the room, so I don't have to worry about someone else changing the sheets and finding the plate.

I let out a laugh.

What the hell am I thinking?

Sure, I can break off a chunk of porcelain. I might even be able to immobilize someone.

But someone else will be right behind him, and someone else behind him. And so on, and so on, and so on.

I don't have a freaking chance in hell of doing any significant damage with a chunk of sharp porcelain, and even if I could, how would I get out of here? I'm on an island, surrounded by the Pacific Ocean. Without help, I'll get nowhere.

And I'll be punished.

I should take the plate back to the common room.

Take it back, put it where it was. Maybe someone else will take it. Someone who's stronger and more knowledgeable than I am.

I secure it safely underneath my mattress. Good thing Emerald isn't here. I'd rather not have to make her keep a secret for me. The less the others know, the better.

Perhaps I can give the plate to someone. Someone with more determination than I have. Someone who can raise an army.

I laugh out loud again.

Right. It'll never happen.

I leave the plate under my mattress, though. It will never be a weapon for me, but I feel a little better just knowing it's there.

~

I SHOOT MY EYES OPEN, still grasping the counter in Luke's kitchenette.

I never made a weapon from the plate.

I never got the chance.

And that plate—that innocuous porcelain plate—turned out to be my undoing.

32

LUKE

Pollack gave me a thirty-five percent tip.

Interesting. He's up to something. Why did he come back to The Glass House if he knew I worked there?

Makes no sense. And now, he gave me a huge-ass tip.

I heaved a sigh of relief that he paid his bill and went on his way.

The rest of the shift went smoothly, and I shared my tip with the bartender. I'm only obligated to hand over twenty percent to the bar, but Pollack's money seems tainted to me in some way.

I don't want it. The rest of it I handed to a guy playing guitar when I walked home at eleven-thirty. Some of the musicians play all night. Probably so they don't have to sleep somewhere and get mugged. They're much better off sleeping during the day. Manhattan has enough of a nightlife that they do all right at night.

I don't need the money, anyway. Sure, I may look like a

waiter who lives in a studio. That's what I'm supposed to look like.

I unlock the door to my place and sneak in. My heart thumps when I look toward the bed. Katelyn is still here. She's asleep, and she looks like an angel.

I close the door behind me, secure the deadbolt, and tread quietly to the bathroom where I wash my hands and face. Normally I shower after work, but I don't want to wake Katelyn.

I shed my clothes, my tattoo catching my attention in the mirror. Damn. Now what? I can't go to bed wearing long sleeves.

Or maybe I can.

I grab a beige Henley—I was told to get neutral clothes that don't stand out—and a clean pair of boxer briefs. Then I slide into my bed next to Katelyn. It's a queen-sized bed, and it takes up quite a bit of space in the small studio. I thought about trading it in for a full, but now I'm glad I didn't. Plenty of room for both Katelyn and me.

I hope this isn't the only time we'll share a bed.

I ache to touch her, run my fingers through her silky golden hair, kiss her milky flesh.

Instead I curl into her body, spooning her.

She tenses against me.

"Hey," I say. "You okay?"

"Luke?"

"Of course it's me. This is my place."

"Right. Right. I was just dreaming."

"Were you? You were still."

"I kind of woke up with a jolt. The dream was... It's...gone. I can't remember."

"That's normal, baby."

"I'm sorry," she says. "I meant to go home."

"Don't be silly. I told you that you could stay."

"I know." She yawns.

I smile. "Sleepy?"

"Yeah. A little."

I kiss the side of her head. "Go to sleep, then, baby. Sweet dreams."

~

I AWAKE WITH A RAGING HARD-ON, of course. I've had one since I got home. Plus, I'm hot and sweaty sleeping in this long-sleeved Henley.

I stumble out of bed quietly, trying not to wake Katelyn. I pad to my tiny kitchen and start a pot of coffee. Then I head to the bathroom to shower. Feels good to get the grime of work off, especially after dealing with Pollack.

I won't tell Katelyn about that. I already know how she knows him, and I'd prefer not to think about it.

I do have a meeting with Anthony DeCarlo at eleven, though, so I need to make some excuse to Katelyn. She can still stay here if she wants to.

I dry off quickly and put on a long-sleeved athletic shirt and blue jeans. Then I pour myself a cup of the coffee that's now done brewing.

My angel still sleeps, her blond hair fanning out on my pillow like a golden curtain. She moves with a soft moan, stretches her arms, and then opens her eyes.

"Hey, sleepyhead," I say.

She smiles. "Hi."

"Coffee?" I hold out my cup.

"Mmm. Not yet. You come here."

I set my coffee down and sit down on the bed. She holds out her arms, and I fall on top of her into her embrace.

There goes my dick again. This "being a good man" stuff is hard on the groin. Big time.

I press my lips to hers, and to my surprise, she parts her lips and welcomes me in. It's a gentle kiss, but only at first. Soon we're both panting and sliding our lips against each other's in a maddening frenzy.

She's wearing only her bra and panties, and I'm fully clothed.

"Please," she sighs into me.

"Katelyn..."

"Please, Luke. There was a time when I thought I'd never want another man. Now that I do, I'm not sure I can take it much longer. I need to remember. I need to know that this thing between a man and a woman can be beautiful too. All I've seen in the past decade is ugly. Show me the beautiful again."

God, her words. Her body. Her sweet and innocent heart. If she only knew who I used to be...

But I'm not him anymore.

I'm Luke Johnson. A good man.

But still a man.

A man who finds Katelyn Brooks impossible to resist.

But how? How can I make love to her with a long-sleeved shirt on?

I'll have to make do, I guess, because the lovemaking is going to happen. And it will be hell to go slowly.

But I'll walk through hell for Katelyn. Today and any day.

It will be nothing compared to what she's been through.

I kiss her cheeks, her neck, the tops of her breasts. She's

so lovely, and when I unclasp the front of her bra, she sucks in her breath but then nods. "It's okay. Please."

The two cups part, and before me is the most perfect set of tits I've ever seen. Slightly larger than my hands, with brown-pink areolas and nipples like berries. Hard and perfect. I kiss around each nipple and then take one between my lips.

She sucks in a breath again.

I look up, and she nods.

All is still good. Thank God.

I play with her nipples using my lips and my fingers, relish in her moans and sighs and *Yes, Luke's*. All the while my cock grows harder, harder, harder, until I'm convinced it's going to break into pieces if it doesn't get inside her soon.

I move downward and pull off her white cotton panties—which are hotter than any lacy thong on any other woman.

Then I slowly spread her legs.

Between them, nestled under her trimmed blond bush, is perfection. Paradise. Pure heaven. I inhale her female musk. It's like a tangy citrus breeze blowing during the Santa Ana winds. A smooth zephyr bringing treats for the nose as well as the eyes.

She's beautiful. Pink and swollen and beautiful.

My cock is so ready. *I'm* so ready. I shimmy out of my jeans and underwear quickly, grab a condom out of the night-stand drawer, and slip it on my dick.

No. Not going to fuck her. Not yet. She deserves more.

"Your shirt, Luke," she whispers.

"Shh," I say. "Not yet."

Then I part her legs farther and lick her slit.

She cries out and grabs two rungs of the headboard. In

my mind's eye, I see her bound there, splayed out for my pleasure.

I'll never bind Katelyn. Already I know this. But my imagination sees a beautiful thing.

"I'm going to lick you, baby. Lick you until you scream."

"I think I already screamed," she says.

"Yeah? You're not done. I'm going to make you feel so good, Katelyn."

"Want... Want...to make you feel good too."

"Oh, you are, baby. And you will."

I dive back between her legs, nibble on her clit for a few seconds and then shove my tongue into her heat, savoring the sweet juices. Damn, if this isn't the sweetest pussy I've ever eaten.

I could eat her forever.

But my cock has other ideas.

I want her to feel something amazing, though, so I continue licking her, sucking on her clit, and then I force a finger inside her tight channel.

"Oh, God! Luke!" She arches her back, lifts her hips, and within seconds she's clamping around my fingers in an enthusiastic orgasm.

"That's it, baby. My sweet Katelyn. Come for me."

She contracts around my fingers, spills more juice over them, and my dick is so ready, so hard I'm convinced it's going to bust through the condom.

She's still coming. I can get inside and savor those pulses.

"Katelyn, I want to come inside you."

"Yes, please. God, Luke."

I crawl atop her and plunge my cock deep inside her heat.

And I'm lost.

Lost in a sea of bliss.

She fits me so perfectly, and my God, she's tight.

Perfect and tight.

She moans beneath me, arches into me, and within a few more thrusts, I'm ready.

So ready.

I release.

And I know I'll never feel this way with another woman.

33

KATELYN

I'm still reeling from my climax when Luke comes inside me.

For the first time in what seems like forever, I want him to stay there. I don't want to run to the shower and rinse the horridness off my body.

No. In fact. I want him to live inside me. My walls are no longer pulsating, but his girth fills an emptiness I never knew was so acute.

An emptiness I never want to feel again.

"God, Katelyn, I—"

I jolt at the harsh ring of my cell phone. Zee asks all the women to keep their phones on the loudest possible setting as part of our security.

"Is that you?" Luke asks.

"Yeah. Sorry. I should get it."

"It's okay, baby." He rolls off me.

It takes all my effort to move the few steps from the bed to the small table where my purse sits. I don't recognize the number.

"Hello?"

"Katelyn? Are you all right?" Zee's frantic voice.

"Zee? Where are you calling from?"

"I'm still in the hospital, waiting for the wheelchair to take me down to the parking lot."

"Oh. That explains why I didn't recognize the number."

"None of this explains where you are," she says. "Security told me you didn't come home last night. I've been worried sick."

My heart falls. The last thing I wanted was to cause anyone any worry. "I'm fine. I'm with..."

"With who, Katelyn? Who are you with?"

"Remember that nice waiter from The Glass House? Luke?"

"Katelyn..."

"I didn't plan this. Neither of us did. And I did talk to Macy about it."

"I'm not here to tell you what to do," Zee says, "and neither is Macy. But you've been through something horrendously traumatic."

"Believe me. I know that. I'm the one who went through it."

"Are you sure you're ready for something like this?"

"No." I let out a nervous laugh. "I'm not sure. Not at all. But is anyone? Ever?"

Silence for a few seconds. Then, "I understand. I probably wasn't ready when Reid and I... You know."

"But you did anyway."

"I did."

"Why?"

"Because"—she clears her throat—"it felt right."

I nod, even though she can't see me. "That's what this

feels like." I look back toward the bed.

Luke is gone. The bathroom door is closed. That's where he went. To give me privacy. What an amazing person. I haven't known true privacy for over a decade.

"Are you sure?"

"Weren't you?"

"Yeah, I was. But I had a much different situation than you did, Katelyn. I got away."

I sigh. She's not wrong. Zee Wolfe is one of the strongest women I've ever met. She got away. She conquered her addiction. Heck, she faced Derek Wolfe and the priest, got them to give her money to start a new life.

That's some amazing strength.

Could I have done it if given the chance?

I'll never know.

All I know is I owe Zee and Reid and the others my life.

"I'm sorry," I say. "I never meant to worry you. I won't do it again."

"You can't make that promise," she says, "not if you truly feel this is right for you."

"He can come to my— Oh, I guess he can't."

"No, he can't. There's a reason why we don't allow men in your building other than security, who are carefully vetted."

"I know. I understand. I'll let you know, then, if I'm going to be gone all night."

She sighs into my ear. "That's not what we want either, Katelyn. We don't want to control you. You're free now. You have the right to live your life as you see fit."

"Then what's the answer?"

Another sigh. "The answer, I guess, is that I need to let you go."

"Maybe I don't want you to let me go."

"We'll still be friends, of course. Maybe I need to tell security not to let me know when someone doesn't come home."

"That's not good. What if there's a problem?"

"I don't have the answer," she says. "Reid and I will talk about it. We'll talk to Macy. Talk to security. We'll figure out a system that works for everyone. Okay?"

The right words don't come to me because I don't know what they are. Having someone checking up on me gives me a sense of security, of safety. But she's right. I *am* free now. I can come and go as I please. I can be with whom I please. I can... I can have sex with a man if I want to, whether I'm emotionally ready for it or not.

"I'll be home soon," I tell her. "I didn't plan this. Otherwise I would have let security know when I left."

"You shouldn't have to do that. This isn't the 1950s, where women have to sign in and out of their college dorms. We're just all very concerned about you and the others."

"I know that, Zee. And I thank you for it."

She inhales. "No need to thank any of us. We're here to help. We *want* to help. I just..."

"What?"

"I feel a responsibility to all of you. I feel...kind of..."

I wait. She's having a hard time saying whatever this is.

"Guilty," she finally says. "I feel guilty. I'm the one who got away. The rest of you didn't. And I feel especially responsible for you, Katelyn. I should have taken you with me. We both could have gotten out."

"We've been through that. There's no way you could have."

Silence again. She knows what I say is true, but she still feels the guilt. I understand. I'd most likely feel the same way.

"You're very special to me," she says.

"You're special to me too." No truer words.

"All right. I'll try to let go a little."

"I'm okay. Enjoy that new baby. I can't wait to see her."

"I'll bring her to the building in a few days," Zee says. "Once we're settled in."

"Sounds great, and I'm so sorry again for worrying you."

"It's all right. Take care, Katelyn. And call me if you need anything. I mean anything."

"I will." I place the phone safely back in my purse.

The bathroom door is still closed, and now I hear the shower. Part of me wants to go into the shower and surprise Luke.

Part of me is scared stiff.

But I can't let fear rule me. I walk slowly to the closed door, let my hand hover over the knob for a moment.

Then I twist it...or attempt to.

It's locked. Locked from the inside.

He locked me out.

Not a huge deal. Most people lock the door when they're in the bathroom.

It bothers me for a fleeting moment and then I get over it.

I do need to get home. I still haven't begun looking for work, and that has to take priority. I search through a few drawers in the kitchenette until I find a pad of paper and pen. I scribble a quick note to Luke, dress quickly, and leave. I don't have a key to lock his deadbolt, but I make sure I lock the smaller lock on the doorknob.

I'm not quite sure where I am, so I hail a cab and give him the address to my place.

Then I smile.

I feel...happy.

Happy is good.

34

LUKE

I turn off the shower and grab a towel. My work clothes hang on the door. I grabbed them when I went into the bathroom. Hiding this tattoo has become work in itself. I need to step up my game and find someone who can remove it—someone who's the best and also who's trustworthy.

I dry off my hair and body, rub antiperspirant under my arms, and spritz on a little cologne. Then I dress and unlock the door.

"Hey," I say, "you hungry?"

No response.

I scan the place—which takes all of two seconds—and I zero in on a piece of paper on the small table where I take my meals.

Luke,

Thank you for a wonderful night. I have some stuff to do this morning. See you soon.

Katelyn

She has stuff to do? Of course. She's looking for work. She told me when we first met. Mental note: check back in with

Lois to see if that hosting position is a possibility. Does Katelyn know how to tend bar? Bartenders are always for hire in New York. Of course, maybe she wants a position with better hours than a restaurant or bar can provide. I can definitely see Katelyn sitting behind a desk doing important things. The things my father wishes I were doing. Or rather, wished I were doing ten years ago instead of what I ultimately chose.

Now the former is impossible.

Those days are gone forever.

I pour myself a cup of coffee and fry a few slices of bacon and two eggs. After my breakfast, I leave the building and hail a cab. Time to pay a visit to Anthony DeCarlo at prison.

～

"WHO THE FUCK ARE YOU?" DeCarlo says into the phone on the other side of the plexiglass.

"Luke Johnson."

"And I'm supposed to know you?"

"No. But we have mutual friends in common."

"Like who?"

"Like the people you give information to, canary."

DeCarlo narrows his eyes. Yup, that got him. I've never actually seen the man, but I know the name. He's got a muscular build and brown eyes. His hair is shaved close to his head, and he's wearing prison beige.

"This some kind of threat?"

"No. No threat. Just letting you know I'm aware of your situation. I'm also betting the reason your parole hearing was canceled wasn't because of a fight you got in."

He narrows his eyes further. "What the hell do you want?"

"I want to know exactly what you did to Katelyn Brooks. And why."

"I don't know what you're talking about, asshole."

"You may want to stop the name-calling, DeCarlo. I promise I can make your life very difficult."

"You? You're nobody."

He's right. I *am* nobody. Or everybody. I'm supposed to blend in. I'm every man. A waiter in Manhattan who lives in a studio.

That's me.

And that's a million other people.

Except I have a past. A past that includes Anthony DeCarlo. A past he's still involved in, even if I'm not.

"Let me rephrase that," I say. "You tell me everything about Katelyn, and if you don't, I'll have the Raven take your head off."

His eyes widen.

The Raven. Even now the words sound foreign. The Raven no longer exists. He never really existed. He was more of an idea than a person. Two words that struck fear in—and apparently still strike fear—in reckless criminal peons like Anthony DeCarlo.

"Now that I have your attention," I say, "Katelyn. Go."

"There's not much to tell. I needed cash. My parish priest said he needed women to serve as nannies for his rich parishioners who didn't want to use undocumented immigrants."

"And that made sense to you? That a priest was so hard up to get young women to be nannies for rich people that he condoned drugging them and taking them?"

"He was a priest, man. Priests are on the up-and-up."

I can't speak for a moment. Really? He's really going to

stay with this fake narrative? "I'm pretty sure I wasn't born yesterday, asshole. I'd like the truth now."

"That is the fucking truth."

I grit my teeth. "Try again."

"What? It's the truth, man. I swear to God."

"You swear to God? Like the good Catholic boy you are, I assume?"

"Fuck you."

Anger scratches at my neck like a bird's talon. "I can have you shivved in your sleep, dickhead, so get moving on the real story. Now."

"I mean it. It was the priest. Father Jim Wilkins. At St. Andrew's in Manhattan. I was an altar boy."

"Was he *that* kind of priest?"

"What the fuck?"

"You know what I'm talking about, DeCarlo. Did he molest you? The altar boys?"

"God, no!" DeCarlo swivels his neck and makes eye contact with a guard.

Shit. I'm nowhere near done with this conversation.

The guard comes forward, and DeCarlo covers the mouthpiece with his hand. I hear murmuring between them, but no discernible words.

As soon as the phone is back on his ear, I say, "Watch your step. We're going to finish this conversation."

"Right," he says. "Yeah."

"I know who owns that guard," I lie, "so what you do is up to you. You may wake up with a knife in your back...if you wake up at all."

He nods, a nervous tick making his lips twitch slightly.

I've learned to take notice of body language. It kept me alive for the last ten years.

"Now...the truth, please."

"It is the truth. The priest said he needed women for nannies, that they wouldn't be harmed, and that he'd pay a lot of fucking cash."

"And you still expect me to believe that you trusted him? Believed this cockamamie story?"

"I was seventeen, man. Seventeen, and goons were threatening me on the daily."

"Now we're getting somewhere. You *didn't* actually believe him."

"I... I wanted to believe him."

"Because he offered you an out."

Silence for a moment.

I narrow my eyes, glare at him.

Finally, "Yeah. He did. I was seventeen. Too young to die."

"They wouldn't have killed you, dumbass. Not until you paid up."

"I know that. Now. But they would have hurt me. Hurt me bad."

"So better Katelyn than you, huh?" Anger wells within me. In my mind's eye, I'm pummeling this dude. Reducing him to mush.

It doesn't escape my thoughts that I've done bad things too. To men. To women.

I'll always carry that with me. The shame. The guilt. But I have a second chance now.

Walk away.

Just fucking walk away.

I should take my own advice. Walk out of here. Let the past go.

But the past...this fucking past... It affects Katelyn, and she's become so important to me.

I never wanted another relationship. I was scared shitless that I'd fall back into my old ways, even if I stayed off the booze.

Walk away, Luke.

My legs don't move, though. My ass stays glued to the uncomfortable plastic chair.

"Yeah," DeCarlo finally admits. "Better her than me. I'm not proud of it."

"And that makes it okay."

God, I'm hating myself right about now. There's so much of my past I'm not proud of. So fucking much. I've atoned. I've put my own life at risk to try to right my wrongs.

But I hurt people—a lot of people, some of whom I thought I cared about—and I can never change that.

"No." He shakes his head. "It doesn't make it okay. I was a kid, man."

"Right. Seventeen. Way too young to understand right and wrong."

I never gave myself a break. Why should I give this idiot one?

"A good churchgoing kid like yourself. You never learned God's lessons. How to treat people. What was inherently good and inherently bad."

"Well, you know the priest I had."

I suppose he's got me there. "The priest who convinced you it was kosher to drug women." I nod. "I'll give you that one. Except you still should have known better."

"Fuck off. I was a kid. I believed my priest. Why do you think some of those pedophile priests get away with shit? Because the kids are conditioned to think the priest can do no wrong. That he knows God's will."

Okay, so he has a point. But, "Those are younger kids. You were only months away from becoming a full-fledged adult."

He bites his lip. Shakes his head. Finally, "I didn't want broken legs, man. I was... I was scared. Fucking scared."

"Yeah. I get it." I get it more than he realizes.

Doesn't change anything, though.

"What the hell made you think of Katelyn?"

"She was young and gorgeous, and no one would miss her for a few months. She was supposed to go to Columbia, so her parents weren't expecting her home any time soon."

"Isn't she your cousin?"

"Second cousin."

"And that makes it better?"

"Hey, it's legal for second cousins to marry. That's not family."

Acid rises in my throat. Did he really just utter those words?

"So if she had been what you consider family, you wouldn't have sold her out. Is that what I'm hearing?"

"This ain't none of your business, whoever the fuck you are."

"Luke. Luke Johnson. Do you want me to repeat it again?"

"How do you know the Raven?"

Again, the invisible talons scrape at my neck.

I don't reply.

He squints at me. "Now that I look a little harder at you, you do look familiar. You're too clean cut, though. No way you're involved in that game. So who the hell are you, Luke Johnson?"

"I'm no one," I say. "Just a person who knows a few people, and a person who cares about Katelyn."

"I already made my peace with Katelyn."

"Oh?"

"Yeah. She came to see me yesterday."

"And she forgave you?"

"Well...no."

"Don't expect that to ever happen."

The truth of my own words spears into my gut. Forgiveness. I'll never have it from those I hurt. I can wish for it. I can even think I deserve it.

But I'll never get it.

And I don't blame those I wronged.

They're perfectly right not to forgive me.

"Listen," I say. "I want the truth, DeCarlo. Did you, at any time, think Katelyn's life would be in danger?"

He shakes his head. "No. I mean, other than having to drug her."

"You thought she'd end up working for some rich family as a nanny to their privileged kids."

"Yes."

"And it never occurred to you that she'd be held against her will."

"No."

"Then why would you have to drug her in the first place? Why not just ask her? Hey, you want to be a nanny for some rich kids?"

"I... This was the way it worked."

"Drugging her meant she'd be held against her will."

"But she wouldn't be harmed."

"Holding someone against her will isn't harming her?"

God, the truth of the words.

I can't. I can't. I can't.

I put the phone back in the holder and stand. DeCarlo lifts his eyebrows. I turn and walk away.

I love Katelyn.

Fuck it all, I love her.

But I can't be with her.

The truth.

The truth of my own words.

The truth is that I'm no better than Anthony DeCarlo.

I'm no one. I'm everyone.

My past no longer matters.

Except that it does.

And I can't get any more deeply involved.

35

KATELYN

I'm back at my place, showered and dressed in navy pants, a white blouse, a string of faux pearls around my neck, when Zee calls again.

"Hi there," I say into the phone.

"Hey. Just got home, and I had a thought."

"Yeah?"

"Reid needs an assistant. His former assistant, Terrence, had to...leave."

"He did?"

"Yeah. Long story that I don't want to get into. But I said to him, 'what about Katelyn?' And my sweet husband said he'd be happy to talk to you."

"Assistant to the CEO—"

"He's the COO, actually. His brother Rock is the CEO."

"Whatever. The top two guys in the company? I'm not qualified, Zee."

"Can you type?"

"Yeah. I mean I learned keyboarding in school just like everyone else."

"Can you read?"

"Zee, what kind of question is that?"

"It's a valid one these days, and I already know you can. You're a smart woman, Katelyn. You can do this."

"I don't know anything about running an office."

"Rock's assistant, Jarrod, will train you. Each office works differently. No matter how much experience you have, you'd need training."

"I have *no* experience. I was on my way to college when all this shit went down, Zee. I have no experience in the real world."

"You don't want an office job?"

"Sure, I'd love an office job. One that I'm qualified for. Something entry level."

A sigh from Zee, and then a cute little oink from the baby. "It's okay, sweetie." Then to me, "I'm nursing, and Nora's having trouble latching on."

"Nora?"

"Yeah. That's our nickname for Honor. My sister-in-law Lacey came up with it."

"Yeah, cute. But Zee—"

"In every business," she says, "it's more about who you know than what you know. Reid is willing to chat with you. You need to take this opportunity, Katelyn."

"But that building..."

The thought of it... The place where I fought for my life, was indeed ready to end my life. It's hard enough to live this close to it.

"I get it. But I live in that building now. The building isn't to blame. The people are. Derek Wolfe, Father Jim, and the others. It was them, not the building. Besides, that underground prison was filled in years ago. It no longer exists."

I sigh. I'd be a fool to let this opportunity slip by. Besides, once I try to do the job, Zee and Reid will both realize they've made a mistake, but maybe I can get some experience under my belt. "Okay, Zee. Thank you."

"Great. Reid wants to talk to you today at two. Can you make it?"

"Sure. What else do I have going on?"

~

THE WOLFE BUILDING.

This is where I was originally held captive. I didn't know it at the time, but this was it. This is where both my shoulders were pulled out of their sockets.

This was where I first met Zee...all those years ago.

I stand in front of it, craning my neck and looking upward. It's massive, like a mirrored monster looking over the city.

It's no Empire State Building or anything like that, but it still looms large in my sight.

Even the biggest buildings can topple.

Look at the World Trade Center.

I inhale a deep breath and walk through the revolving doors. I stop at reception.

"May I help you?" a young woman, Bluetooth lodged in her ear, asks.

"I have an appointment with Mr. Wolfe."

"Mr. Rock Wolfe or Mr. Reid Wolfe?"

"I'm sorry. Reid."

"Name?"

"Katelyn Brooks."

She nods and speaks into her Bluetooth. "Katelyn Brooks

for Mr. Reid Wolfe." Pause. "Thank you. I'll send her up." She hands me a small card. "The elevators are to your right. Follow the instructions on the card and check in with reception up there." She hands me a tag that says visitor. "Clip this on."

I lift my eyebrows and then notice two security guards.

"The Wolfes take security very seriously," the receptionist says.

"Right." I clip the tag to my blouse. "Thank you."

Once in the elevator, my stomach is flopping. I'm not sure it's because the elevator is going very fast, which it is, or because of the interview I have with Reid.

Reid loves his wife. If Zee wants me in this position, I will probably get it.

Do I want it?

Sure.

Can I do it?

That's another question altogether.

The elevator stops, jolting my stomach back into place. the doors slide open and I step out cautiously. Glass walls meet me. *Wolfe Enterprises* is etched in serif lettering.

I gather my courage, open the glass door, and walk in toward another reception desk.

"Good morning," a receptionist, this one a young man, says.

"Hi. I'm here to see Reid Wolfe." I swallow, trying not to feel as nervous as I am. "Katelyn Brooks."

"Just a minute, please." He talks into his Bluetooth just like the lobby receptionist, except this time I'm not listening.

I'm gazing at the waiting area. A sculpture of an Arabian horse sits in the corner next to a ficus. Leather couches and chairs surround a large marble coffee table that's piled with books on Renaissance art, the state of Montana, and Harley Davidson motorcycles.

An odd combination.

"Have a seat," the receptionist says, nodding toward the area. "Mr. Wolfe will be a few minutes. Can I get you some coffee or water? A soft drink?"

I shake my head. Anything that goes down is going to come right back up at this moment.

And it nearly does when Reid Wolfe walks into the reception area, a smile on his handsome face. He's dressed impeccably in a navy suit with a red silk tie, his dark hair short and styled. The man could be walking a runway.

"Good afternoon, Katelyn. Come on back."

36

LUKE

I can't catch my breath.

Fuck! What's wrong with me? I somehow make it out of the visiting area, out of the prison. Cab. I need a cab to get home. Or to work. Where am I going? I grab my phone to check the time, but the screen is blurred.

God, get a grip!

I walk away from the building and then turn.

But for the grace of God, I'd be behind these very walls. Not these actual walls, but the walls of a prison somewhere in California.

Am I any better than Anthony DeCarlo?

Than Derek Wolfe?

Are there degrees of evil?

Derek Wolfe was evil. That priest was evil.

Tony DeCarlo? I can't see him as evil. He's a normal guy who got involved with some bad people and made some bad decisions. He's paying for it.

But damn. Katelyn paid more for it. How many others did he "give" to that priest?

I should have asked him. I should have found out so much more.

Anthony DeCarlo isn't all that different from the man I used to be. Sure, I can blame the alcohol, but no one poured it down my throat, forced me to swallow it. I can blame my old man, but no one made me leave home and go underground. No one held me at gunpoint.

I did it.

I did it all.

And only *I* bear the responsibility.

I treated people badly. I treated women badly. I never drugged anyone, but I inflicted damage.

And the only reason I'm alive today is because...

Fuck!

I can't think about it. My phone screen gradually comes into focus and I order a cab to meet me outside the prison.

You can find a cab instantly in most of New York City, but apparently not in front of an upstate prison. Can't blame the cabbies. Who the hell wants to hang around a prison?

I stumble to a bench and sit down to wait for the cab.

But for the grace of God.

That's BS and I know it. It wasn't the grace of God that saved me from a lifetime behind bars.

It was my father.

My old man, who's no longer a part of my life.

I used to long for this day, and now... Now I want his advice. I want to see him. More than him, I want to see my mother. My beautiful mother who, even after the life I chose, refused to turn her back on her firstborn son.

No one would have blamed her if she'd written me off.

Hell, even *I* wouldn't have blamed her.

But she didn't.

So here I am. A new life. A new start. A new everything.

I'm no one and I'm everyone.

Luke Johnson. Every man.

I don't like to think about how this all happened, about what this new start cost me. I don't care about that old life anymore, but I do care about those I harmed, and I do care what I had to do to leave it.

Canary. I called DeCarlo a canary.

When right here, inside my own skin, is the worst canary of all.

Funny how things become so much more clear when no alcohol clouds my thoughts. When I actually allow myself to consider my actions, consider their effect on others.

I'm not proud of my past, and I wish...

I wish I truly *were* Luke Johnson, no man and every man.

I wish I were because then I could have Katelyn. I'd be free to give her the kind of relationship she deserves. I'd be free to protect her.

Free to love her.

To fucking love her.

I've always been quick to fall in love, except it wasn't actually love. It was obsession. I learned through therapy that alcohol was part of what made me that way, and the first step to change my obsessive ways with women was to get off the sauce.

I did it.

But am I going the same route with Katelyn?

That's the question I must answer, and to answer it, I must be honest with myself.

I was a powerful man in LA. A powerful and corrupt man. I can blame the alcohol to an extent. I can blame my father to an extent.

But the ultimate blame rests on my own shoulders.

I grew addicted not only to alcohol, but to the power I wielded.

And with that power, I became abusive.

I pull up the camera on my phone and look at myself. The sun is out, and a glare punctuates my face. My hair is cut short and is so dark brown it's almost black. My eyes are brown as well. A normal everyday color.

The long sleeves of my shirt cover the tattoo that used to define me.

Also underneath my shirt are scars. A bullet in my shoulder. I knife wound to my abdomen. And one to the back.

From a woman.

Luke Johnson has short dark hair and brown eyes.

But through the façade I see the real me. The long blond hair, the blue eyes, and the tattoo that starts on the back of my left hand and travels up my arm and across my left shoulder.

The tattoo that—even after laser removal—will always be with me. I'll always see it, just like the hair dye and colored contact lenses can't change me.

Perhaps I'm still him.

Perhaps I always will be.

A yellow cab skids to a stop.

I hop in. "The Glass House in Manhattan."

I don't have time to go home, which is why I wore my work clothes. I'll be a little early for my shift, but that's good. It'll give me something to think about other than my fucked-up life.

I thought I could do this.

I pull out my phone, go to contacts, pull up my mother.

I could call her so easily. Just touch the screen, and she'd answer in her soft and comforting voice.

So easy...

I slam the phone back into my pocket.

No. I can't ruin this. People put their lives on the line to give me my current circumstances.

I can't let them down.

More than that... I can't let Katelyn down.

Katelyn. The woman I love. The woman I don't have the urge to control. Which means...

Which means it's probably real love this time.

Real fucking love.

And the best thing I can do for her is to let her get on with her new life—the life she deserves.

Without me.

37

KATELYN

I'm fidgeting with my fingers as Reid leads me not to his private office but to a small conference room.

"Have a seat." He holds out a chair and then sits down adjacent to me. A laptop is open in front of him, and another woman sits across from me—short dark hair, friendly brown eyes. "Katelyn, meet Alicia Davis, my personal secretary."

I begin to stand but Alicia simply reaches across the table to shake my hand. "So nice to meet you, Katelyn. Mr. Wolfe speaks very highly of you."

I clear my throat. "Thank you. Nice to meet you too."

"Alicia is going to take notes during our interview," Reid says, "and she's also here because if you choose to take the position as my assistant, you and she will be working together closely."

If I choose to take the job? Does that mean I already have it? That can't be.

"Our company," Reid continues, "is committed to helping all of my father's victims make the transition into healthy and productive lives. If we can help by employing them, all the better."

"That's very kind of you."

"It's the least we can do. My wife, as you know, feels very strongly about this as well. You're one of her favorites, Katelyn."

My cheeks warm. "Thank you. I owe her everything. I owe all of you everything."

"We feel that we owe you. It was our father who put you in danger, who stole years of your young lives."

"None of that is your fault."

"We know that," Reid says, "but we all wonder if perhaps we should have been more vigilant. If we had, maybe we could have found out what our father was up to long ago."

"Don't blame yourself, please. It's the last thing I want."

"You're very kind, Katelyn, and I appreciate that. I'm not so sure all my father's victims feel the same way, and to be honest, I can't blame them if they don't. Let's get down to business, then.

"Of course."

"My assistant needs to work closely with Alicia. You'll handle my calendar. You'll sit in on all meetings and take notes. You'll do a lot of traveling with me."

"If I may ask, what is the difference between your assistant and your secretary?"

Alicia smiles.

Crap. Did I just make a humongous faux pas? I was eighteen years old when I was taken. I haven't experienced any of life. Which means I'm not qualified for this job, and I have no clue how to conduct myself during an interview.

"Alicia's main responsibilities are typing up documents,

filing, mailing, taking phone calls. As an executive assistant, you would be her immediate supervisor."

My cheeks warm. "Wouldn't Alicia be a better person for this job? I could be a secretary."

Alicia smiles. "Mr. Wolfe and I talked about that, actually, and I'm happy where I am. I'm not comfortable in a supervisory position."

"Plus, Alicia has the fastest fingers in New York." Reid laughs. "I doubt you could match her keyboarding skills."

"I'm sure I couldn't, since I haven't touched a keyboard in ten years."

"How would you feel about supervising?"

"I...don't know. I've *been*...supervised for the last ten years."

"Katelyn"—Reid's countenance gets very serious—"the last ten years don't matter here. Okay? You need to believe that. They are not your fault, and they have no bearing on your qualifications for this job."

"I'm sorry, Mr. Wolfe, but they do. I can't help saying that. I don't have the first clue how to be anyone's assistant. Let alone executive assistant to the COO of a major enterprise. I would love to work here. Truly. But let me start at the bottom and prove myself first."

Alice smiles. "I have to say, Katelyn, I already like you a lot."

"If that's what you prefer," Reid says, "but Zee really wants you working here in the office with me. She feels you're a perfect candidate, and I think she may be right."

"With all due respect, why?"

"Because you're an intelligent young woman. You're strong, and you learn quickly. You're dependable. You completed every task asked of you at the retreat center without complaint."

"Didn't everyone?"

Reid lets out a chuckle. "No. Everyone did not. Some of the women fought it every step of the way. That's not their fault. They just had more trouble getting past what happened to them, which is certainly understandable. But you... You were different. You, Lily, Aspen, and Kelly are the only women so far who have left the retreat center."

"Why not ask one of them to take this position?"

"Because Zee asked me to consider you first."

"So because I'm friends with your wife..."

"Yup." He smiles. "A little nepotism never hurt anyone. Plus, I happen to agree with Zee on this, and Alicia and I have spoken about it as well."

"We have," Alicia says. "I believe you can do this job, Ms. Brooks."

"Katelyn, please."

Alicia smiles. "Of course. Katelyn."

"Let's do this," Reid says. "Let's put you to work on a trial basis for two weeks. If you feel you can't handle the responsibilities of the position, you can walk away after two weeks. At the same time, if I'm not satisfied with your work, I can let you go after two weeks. Does that sound fair?"

I swallow, will my head to nod. "All right. I hope I'm worthy of your confidence in me."

"I think you are," he says, "but if you're not, I'll tell you. I'm nothing if not honest. Of course, I'll then have to deal with a new mother at home." He smiles.

"I really don't want—"

He holds up his hand. "I'm kidding, Katelyn. Zee wants me to have the best help possible. She thinks that's you. It may well be, but it may not be. The only way we'll know for sure is to try. Right?"

I nod. It's easier this time. "Right."

"Great. I'll expect you first thing Monday morning at eight o'clock. Alicia will take you down to HR now to get all your paperwork completed." He stands and holds out his hand. "Welcome to the team."

I rise as well and take his outstretched hand with my own clammy one. "Thank you. For everything."

Alicia rises as well. "Come with me. I'll show you to HR."

I smile at her and follow.

And hope like hell I haven't bitten off way more than I can chew.

38

LUKE

Friday nights are busy at The Glass House, and I'm grateful for the distraction. I got here early, and Lois put me straight to work getting both dining rooms ready. Not usually my job, but I don't care. Anything to keep from thinking about who I used to be.

And what it's costing me.

Katelyn.

I can't have Katelyn.

No relationships for me. I'm reduced to casual hookups. No falling in love. I can't risk it.

Despite having never waited tables—hell, I never had to work if I didn't want to—I'm good at this. Great, actually. All those years of keeping numbers in my head have paid off. Tonight I forgot to stick a pad in my apron pocket, and I memorized all the orders from my first round of tables. I got them all perfect.

So now I'm one of those waiters who doesn't carry a pad. Feels pretty good, actually, though the crap is still lurking in the back of my mind.

Me. My old life. What it's costing me now.

Katelyn.

I look toward one of my tables that has just been seated—
My heart jumps.

Katelyn sits at the two-top with another woman I don't recognize. I'm good with faces, but I don't think she's been in here before. The Glass House is hard to get into, so they must have had this reservation in advance.

I could trade tables with Travis.

Good idea.

I grab him as he whisks by. "Hey, I need to trade a table with you. Number sixty-seven."

"Sixty-seven's a two-top."

"So? Give me another two-top."

"I don't have one right now."

"Crap. I'll give you the tips for the trade, then. I just can't do sixty-seven."

Travis glances over my shoulder toward the table. "A couple hotties? What's the problem, Luke?"

"I just can't."

"Fine with me. You take the foursome at twenty-three, and I'll take care of the ladies." He raises an eyebrow.

"Easy. They're customers, not cheesecakes in a bakery window."

He laughs and walks toward Katelyn's table. I saunter toward the middle-aged foursome who are seated at twenty-three, no pad in hand. I take their drink orders quickly and drop them off at the bar, turn, and—

Travis juts into my path. "Hey, Luke. No deal."

"What do you mean no deal?"

"I mean they want you. Apparently they requested seating in your section."

Fuck. "Tell them I switched sections."

"You don't think that's the first thing I said? They asked me to get the manager. Lo's talking to them now."

"Fuck it all." I rub my forehead. "And here she comes."

Lois approaches us briskly. "I don't know what you're up to, Luke, switching tables with Travis, but those two ladies want you to serve them. Are they friends of yours?"

"Not really. One of them was with Zee Wolfe when she went into labor. Remember?"

"Right. Now I recognize her. The blonde. So what's the problem?"

"Nothing. I just owed Travis a favor. Now he owes me one." I glare at him.

"Hey, man, none of this is my fault," Travis says. "I owe you nothing."

"You owe *me* something," Lois says. "Get back to work. Both of you." She touches my forearm a little more than casually.

I pretend not to notice and head straight to Katelyn's table. "Hi, Katelyn."

She beams. God, she's beautiful. "Luke, guess what?"

"What?"

"Oh, I'm sorry. This is Alicia. Alicia, Luke."

The other woman is attractive—short hair and a girl-next-door vibe—but nothing compared to Katelyn.

"Hi, Luke," she says. "Nice to meet you. Katelyn's told me all about you."

"You have?"

"Of course! I have some great news. Alicia and I are celebrating."

"Oh? Celebrating what?"

"My new job. I'm going to work at Wolfe Enterprises as

Reid Wolfe's assistant. Alicia is his personal secretary, so we'll be working together closely."

Just as well. As much as I thought having Katelyn working at The Glass House was a good idea a couple days ago, now I'm glad it's not happening. No way can I leave her if I see her every day.

"Congratulations. That's great news."

Katelyn frowns slightly. "I thought you'd be happier."

I force a smile. "Of course I am! It's great."

"I wanted to come here to celebrate, but I called and the host said you were booked. But then Reid called for us." She beams. "I guess when you know the right people..."

I nod. "It's not what you know. It's who you know." I hate the words that come out of my mouth. I got through the first thirty-three years of my life because of who I knew.

Because of who I *was*.

Kind of makes me sick to think about it.

"What can I get started for you, ladies?"

"A bottle of bubbly, I think," Alicia says.

"That's too much," Katelyn replies.

"Actually, Reid told me to order it. Unless you don't like Champagne, of course."

"Who doesn't like Champagne?" Katelyn laughs. "I haven't had any in... I'm honestly not sure I've ever had any, to tell you the truth."

"Then we have to have it," Alicia says. "What do you recommend, Luke?"

Ask me to recommend Champagne? I can do that. "I no longer drink alcohol, but I personally think the best is Dom Perignon."

"Dom Perignon it is, then," Alicia says. "And the Beluga caviar."

"Caviar?" Katelyn says.

"Yes. Reid said to order it." She turns to me. "He would have come with us but he wanted to get home to Zee and the baby."

I simply nod. Is Reid Wolfe footing this bill? Already it's over six hundred dollars. Alicia probably has an expense account.

So will Katelyn.

I groan inwardly.

She's about to enter a lifestyle that I left behind.

All the more reason why we can never work.

My heart breaks just thinking about it.

"Good enough. The sommelier will bring your wine."

"Aren't you going to write it down?" Katelyn asks me.

"Nah. I'll remember." I turn and walk swiftly away from table sixty-seven, put the wine order in with the sommelier, and the caviar order in with the sous chef.

I do a quick check-in with my other tables and then walk briskly through the kitchen and outside to the alley.

I need some air.

My mutt is there, scraping at the ground. "Hey, Jed. You hungry, boy?" I walk back into the kitchen and grab one of the assistant chefs. "You got any meat scraps? Bones?"

"Check the composter," he says.

"Thanks, man." I grab two fresh bones, both with substantial meat on them, and head back out to the alley.

"Here you go, boy." I hand Jed one of the bones.

He takes it and lies down.

Glad I could make *someone's* night. I lean against the brick wall.

This alley...

This is where I kissed Katelyn for the first time. Where I felt something new and exciting for the first time.

Something special.

Am I really going to let that go?

What if I *can* truly change? What if I can truly be Luke Johnson, not only in name but in all ways?

What if I can truly leave everything else behind?

That was the idea from the beginning. In fact, if I don't, I'll be in danger. Constant danger.

Danger I *cannot* inflict on Katelyn. Not on anyone, but especially not her after what she's been through.

Fuck.

I could really use a drink right now.

I slide my back down the brick wall, probably snagging my cotton shirt. Jed is busy with his bone. I pet him on his head, which is soft despite the fact that he needs a bath badly.

"Good boy. That's a good boy."

I'd take him home, but my place doesn't allow pets.

"You and I have something in common," I say to my canine friend. "Neither of us belongs here. Of course, that's where our similarities end. You deserve a nice home with people who love you, a full belly, and a warm bed. I don't deserve any of that."

Jed chews on his bone, oblivious to the fact that life could be so much better for him.

In that moment, I wish I were a dog.

39

KATELYN

"You were right," Alicia says to me. "He *is* gorgeous."

"Yeah, but he's acting a little weird."

"He's just busy. Look around. This place is hopping tonight."

Alicia's not wrong. But Luke isn't hustling to and from his tables. He seems to have disappeared.

I clear my throat. "Could you excuse me a moment? I need to use the ladies' room."

"Of course." Alicia takes a sip of her water.

I rise and head toward the back where the restrooms are but then take a detour to the staff lounge. I open the door and peek in. A man and woman are inside, chatting. A server and busboy on break. "Oops. Sorry. Wrong door." I close it.

Where did Luke go?

Then I remember. Our kiss. The alley. Except I have to go through the kitchen to get there. I hold my head high and walk into the kitchen. Workers are bustling around, all busy, so no one seems to notice me.

Nicely done, Katelyn.

I step into the alley and—

"Luke. There you are."

He's sitting on the ground petting a stray dog—a cute furry guy with short light hair—when he looks up. "What are you doing out here?"

"Looking for you."

He stands quickly. "Did you need something? I put the orders in. The sommelier should be delivering your Dom right about now."

"I just wanted to talk to you. You seem a little...off."

"Off?"

"Yeah. I guess I expected you to be as excited as I am about the job opportunity."

He smiles, though it seems weak. "I'm very happy for you. Of course I am."

I force my lips into a weak smile to match his. "Really?"

"Yeah."

"You don't sound—"

He advances on me, his eyes full of flame. "All I really want, at this moment, is to kiss you, Katelyn."

"Plea—"

But before the word is complete his lips are on mine, and he's taking me. Ravishing me with his mouth.

Luke's kisses are something so special, so hypnotic. He doesn't just kiss. He makes love with his mouth. He fucks with his mouth.

I'm throbbing all over, especially between my legs.

Can you climax from a kiss? I'm beginning to think it's possible.

Just as I'm sure I'm about to find out, he breaks the kiss with a loud smack. "Let's get out of here."

"Luke, I—"

"I need you. I need to have you one more time. Please."

"One more time? What are you—"

"Please, baby. Please."

Yes. God I want to say it. I want him so badly. But—

"I'm on a business dinner, Luke. You know that. And you're working."

"I don't give a damn. Please, Katie. Please."

Katie? No one's called me Katie since...

Aunt Agnes two days ago.

And Jared, that night...

"Don't call me that," I say.

His eyes widen. "Katie? Okay. Katelyn, then. Baby. My angel."

I sigh. *My angel.*

I want to melt into him, kiss him again, feel his hard body against mine—all hard to my soft.

I want him inside me—not just joined in bodies but I want him inside my soul.

Except he already is.

I never imagined I could feel this way after what I've been through. Never imagined in a million years.

"Please, baby. I don't care about my job. I just need *you.* I need you, Katelyn."

"I can't." I push at his chest, force myself away from him. "I just got his job. Reid is counting on me, giving me a chance."

"This is dinner with his secretary, not a work day with him. Please."

"What about your—"

He presses his lips to mine. "I don't care about that. All I care about is you. Just you."

"If you care about me, then you care about this dinner."

He inhales, backs up until he hits the brick walls, slides into a sitting position, and strokes the dog's head once more. "I do understand. You're right. Go back to your dinner."

"What about you? You have a job to do tonight."

"Right. You're right."

"You'll be back, then? To take our order?"

"You'll be taken care of."

I reach down and stroke his cheek. "See you inside."

I walk into the kitchen. This time I get a few strange looks, but no one asks what I'm doing there. I make a beeline to the ladies' room and wash my hands. Then back to the table.

The champagne sits in a silver ice bucket next to our table, and two flutes are poured.

"Hey," Alicia says. "I was beginning to think you fell in."

"I'm fine. Just a little tummy ache."

She frowns. "I'm sorry. Do you want to postpone our dinner?"

Hmm... If I postpone the dinner, I can give Luke what we both want.

No. I'm not going to begin my new career by being unprofessional and lying to my co-worker.

Though I already lied about the stomachache.

That's as far as my lying will go. Plus I don't want to be responsible for Luke losing his job here. He'll see reason. I look around. He isn't in the dining room yet, at least not that I can see.

Alicia picks up her flute. "To you and your new career path."

I clink my glass to hers. "Thanks." I take a sip and smile as the bubbles tickle my tongue. I let them sit there for a moment, reveling in the dry citrus and woodsy flavor.

I think I like Champagne.

I swallow. "Wow. Delicious."

"It is. One nice fringe benefit of working with the Wolfes is the amazing dinners we get treated to. They're really good to their employees."

"They're just good people," I reply.

"They are. And I'm so sorry, Katelyn, for everything you went through."

"Did you know him? Derek Wolfe?"

She takes another sip. "Yes, but not well. He stayed in his own office for the most part and Reid went to him. I was often there to take notes if Terrence wasn't available."

"Terrence was his prior assistant?"

"Yeah. Recommended by Mr. Wolfe senior. That didn't end well."

"I'm sorry."

"Don't be. I don't know the details, but I think Terrence was probably on Derek's private payroll. Besides, if he were still here, you wouldn't have this job."

I sigh. "Alicia, I'm completely unqualified. I hope I don't disappoint you and Mr. Wolfe."

"You won't. Reid's a great guy, but he's a businessman at heart. If he didn't think you had the brains to learn the job and do it well, he wouldn't have hired you, no matter what Zee wanted."

"You think?"

"I know. Don't get me wrong. Reid has a total soft spot for Zee, who's amazing, by the way."

"I know. I literally owe her my life."

Alicia nods. "But even since Zee came into his life, Reid has been all business. They're getting ready to put the final touches on the resort on the island, so he's been really busy. They hope to open within six months."

"The retreat center and art colony are already open."

"True. They were able to use existing buildings for those so they opened sooner. They just needed staff. But the resort is going to be first class all the way. The ultimate luxury getaway."

I widen my eyes. "On that island…"

"I know it must seem horrible to you, but the Wolfes wanted to take back the island. Turn it into something good. So they came up with the retreat center, run by Riley Wolfe Rossi."

Riley. Derek's daughter. Who he… I shake my head to clear it. "The model. Right."

"The model who was also horribly abused by her father. She wants to help her father's other victims and others who would benefit from therapy and counseling in the backdrop of a tropical island. Then the art colony for Roy and his wife, Charlie. They're both artists. Rock and Reid are the businessmen, so they're profit-driven, of course. The luxury resort and casino is their baby."

"Still…that island…"

"I get it. I do. I don't expect that you or any of the other women will ever go back there again."

"I'd have stayed longer at the center if it were somewhere else."

"Riley understands that. That's why she put together the complex you live in. Zee, who was also a victim of Derek, as you know, will be spearheading that. After maternity leave, of course."

I nod. I know all this. I never met Riley while I was at the retreat center, but we all heard her tragic and inspiring story. Riley's not a counselor. She's not qualified, and neither is her husband, so they left our recovery to the professionals.

"Alicia..."

"Yeah?"

"I don't want to talk about my past, if that's okay with you."

"Oh! Of course. I was just—"

I hold up a hand. "You don't have to explain yourself. I'm trying to take life one day at a time, and I'm dealing with everything in my own way."

"Like getting involved with our hot waiter?"

Warmth spreads across my cheeks. "We've only been out a couple times."

"You go as slowly as you need to go. Or as quickly. Everyone recovers in her own way."

"You seem to know what you're talking about. Have you been through...something?"

"Nothing like what you've been through, but I've struggled with mental health. It's a priority for me, and for everyone at Wolfe Enterprises. They'll take care of you." She glances at her menu as a server arrives with our caviar.

A server who isn't Luke.

"Here you go, ladies. Beluga caviar with blini." He sets the lovely display between us on the table.

I stare at him. His nametag says Travis. He's tall and attractive—brown hair and hazel eyes, a lazy smile—but he's not Luke.

"What happened to Luke?" I ask.

"He had to leave early. Something came up. But don't you worry. You're in good hands. My name is Travis and it will be my pleasure to take care of you this evening."

"Is Luke all right?" I ask breathlessly.

"He's fine. Just had to go. Do you ladies have any questions about the menu?"

"Uh...no."

"We have two specials tonight," Travis says. "One is a New York strip seared with mustard butter, side of mashed potatoes and fresh green beans, and the other..."

The words become incomprehensible to me.

Luke.

I just saw him. He wanted me to leave with him.

I should have gone.

Worry niggles at me.

What's going on with him?

That kiss. That raw kiss full of need and emotion. In my mind's eye I see us—our bodies pressed together, our arms and legs tangled and wrapped around each other.

And he enters me as he kisses me—those firm and drugging kisses.

Katelyn?

My eyelids grow heavy.

Katelyn?

"Katelyn?"

My eyes pop open. "Yeah?"

"You were a million miles away," Alicia says. "Do you want to order?"

"Oh. Yeah. Sure. I'll have the pasta."

"Which one?" Travis asks.

There's more than one? I glance down at the menu. "The penne arrabiata."

"Great." Travis makes a note. "Enjoy that caviar, ladies. It's the best."

I stare as Travis hustles away. Luke gave up our table—our table and a huge tip, with the Dom Perignon and the caviar.

"You okay?" Alicia asks.

"Yeah. Fine. Just thinking about some stuff."

"That's my fault," she says. "I'm sorry I brought all that up."

"It's okay. I don't want people walking on eggshells around me. I could tell you about my life before, but it's pretty boring. I was eighteen when I was taken."

Alicia winces. "Sorry."

"Don't be. It *should* make you uncomfortable. It's a terrible, terrible thing."

"I can imagine."

No, you can't. I don't say this, of course. It's not Alicia's fault that she truly can't imagine. It sure wouldn't make me happier if she could. I'm glad she can't. I'm glad only very few of us can.

I clear my throat. "Tell me about yourself. How long have you been with Reid?"

"A couple years. I love it. He's a great boss."

I nod. "I'm sure."

"We were all shocked when he married Zee so quickly. He was the quintessential bachelor. Kind of a womanizer. A different piece of arm candy at every event. You know the type."

"Reid? Really?" I shake my head. The man is devoted to Zee. They're about as in love as any two people I've ever seen.

Of course, I haven't seen a lot of lovebirds in the last ten years.

Shit. Lovebirds. Why did that word come to mind?

Lovebird.

I blink, trying to make Alicia less blurry, as a movie plays in my mind.

A movie best left forgotten.

~

"I'm in love with you, Moonstone. You're my lovebird."

I smile, purr the way he likes. He hurts me less when I'm accommodating.

What this derelict doesn't seem to understand is that if he were truly in love with me, he wouldn't beat me with a yardstick. He wouldn't rape me.

At least he doesn't hunt me.

Only one of my regulars likes the hunt. The rest just like to hurt me, humiliate me.

Still, Lovebird humiliates me less than Ice Man, who never touches me except with his urine. Lovebird whispers sweet nothings in my ear. Tells me how much he loves me as he forces himself on me.

That's so not love.

I'll never experience love.

What will happen when I grow old and I'm no longer attractive to the kind of men who come here to Treasure Island? Will I end up like Diamond? She was beautiful once. I see it in her eyes. But now she's old and tired and broken.

I haven't seen any woman leave the island. But Turquoise is older than the rest of us. She already has laugh lines around her eyes. Where did they come from? We don't laugh here.

We never laugh.

Later, after Lovebird leaves, Diamond gives me a pill for the pain on my back and ass. I pretend to swallow it.

I'm not going to be strung out on narcotics like some of the women are. I'll gladly bear the pain. Those two dislocated shoulders were about as painful as anything I've felt, and I got through them without meds.

"He broke skin in a few places," Diamond says. "Let me clean you up."

"I'm fine."

"You're not fine." She sighs. "You're not fine, Moonstone."

I turn to her then. "Who are you, Diamond? Who are you really?"

She sighs again. "I'm no one. The same as you, Moonstone. I'm no one."

B ack at my place, I begin packing.

I got Travis and another server to cover me by telling them I had an emergency. I didn't bother to tell Lois I was leaving. She has a giant crush on me and would ask a lot of questions. Travis and Marguerite just wanted my tables and their tips. They were too busy to question my motives.

Not the most professional thing I've ever done, but what the hell? I'm out of here.

A leopard doesn't change its spots.

Wisdom from my old man.

I was determined to prove him wrong.

The problem? I can't prove him wrong as Luke Johnson. No man and every man.

Luke Johnson doesn't exist.

I have to prove him wrong as myself. Only then will I deserve Katelyn and her love.

And I *do* love her.

Not the obsessive love I felt for the others, but a more

profound love. I want what's best for her over what's best for myself.

I've never felt that before. I always put my own desires first.

No more.

I may not come out alive, but if I do, I will finally be worthy of Katelyn.

I remove my white shirt and stuff it in the suitcase.

No more hiding. The tattoo screeches at me. Even if I go through with removal, the shadow of it will always exist. Inside me. Part of me.

Some things will never leave my psyche.

I step into the bathroom and regard myself. A stranger I've come to know stares back at me. Luke Johnson has dark hair and dark eyes. Luke Johnson always wears long sleeves.

Luke Johnson—

Buzz.

Someone's downstairs. Who the hell is coming to see me at eight p.m.? I didn't order food.

Doesn't matter. I'm out of here as soon as I'm packed up.

Buzz.

This stranger is persistent.

Buzz. Buzz. Buzz.

"All right! I'm coming!" I grab the crumpled white shirt out of my suitcase and shove my arms back into it, not bothering to button it up.

"Yeah? What do you want?" I say harshly into the intercom.

"Luke?"

Damn. Katelyn. I'd recognize her angelic voice anywhere. Just what I *don't* need.

Except I'm lying. I *do* need her. I need her so badly.

I'm just not worthy of her.

"I'm busy," I say, wincing at my own words.

"I just want to make sure you're all right."

"I'm fine."

"Uh...okay. Can I... Can I come up?"

"Katelyn, that's not a good—"

"Oh, thank you." Katelyn's voice.

The intercom goes dead.

Someone opened the door, and Katelyn is on her way up.

I don't have to open the door. I can tell her to get lost. But already I know I won't do that. She'll be right outside my door in the few minutes it take her to get up here.

God, I ache for her. Ache so badly.

A hesitant knock.

I throw open the door.

She stands, still in her professional clothes, her gorgeous blond hair tumbling over her shoulders, her lips red and parted.

So ready for my tongue to slide between them.

"Hi," she says hesitantly.

"Come in."

She steps inside and I close the door.

Her gaze falls to the suitcase on my bed. "What's this?"

"I'm getting out of town for a few days."

"Oh? Where are you going?"

"To visit family." Not a complete lie.

She nods and bites her lower lip. Man, I wish I were her teeth.

"Is there some kind of emergency?" she asks. "You left the restaurant without finishing your shift."

I clear my throat. "Yeah. An emergency."

Lies used to come so easily past my lips. Now? I taste bile

and acid as I spew them. I don't want to lie to Katelyn. Not ever. But the fact is that I've been lying to her since we met. I'm not who she thinks I am, and I never will be.

"What happened?" she asks. "Is everyone all right?"

"Yeah, fine. Just...my mother needs me."

"Oh. Sure. I understand. But..."

"But what?"

"Weren't you going to at least say goodbye?"

I itch to reach out to her, to caress her silky cheek, to trail my finger over those full parted lips.

To grab her. Kiss her senseless. Make love to her all night long.

I was ready before. I begged her to leave the restaurant with me. And now? She's here. Ready for the taking.

I walk toward her, the two sides of my shirt hanging and baring my chest to her. She's never seen my chest. I wore a Henley when we made love.

Perhaps it's time. I'm leaving anyway.

Perhaps she should see who I really am. No more hiding. As soon as I leave this apartment for the last time, I'll no longer be Luke Johnson.

I slowly work my arms out of the shirt.

Her eyes widen. "Luke..."

"I love you."

The words surprise me. They're completely true, but they erupted out of my throat with barely a thought.

She reaches toward me, touches my chest, gazes at the tattoo that travels up my left arm. "My God. You're beautiful."

I haul her to me and crush my lips to hers. They're already parted, so I dive in. I kiss her with untamed passion, with all the love I feel for her.

I kiss her as though it's the last time...

Because it may very well be.

I inch backward toward my bed and let go of her just long enough to push my open suitcase onto the floor. The clothes spill out, but I don't care. I'll deal with it later.

Right now I have Katelyn in my arms.

And for the next couple hours, until my bus leaves at midnight, I'm going to take her.

Make love to her while we're both naked, let her see me as I am, and I'll see her as she is.

The lights will stay on, and I'll make every second count.

Because I'll need this memory to get me through what's to come.

41

KATELYN

I forewent dessert at dinner with Alicia so I could get to Luke faster. I wasn't hungry anyway after he left so abruptly. The caviar tasted like salty mush, and my pasta was flavorless. I smiled and nodded while Alicia drove our conversation, and as soon as we were out of the restaurant, I hailed a cab and asked the driver to bring me here.

I should be angry at Luke. Angry that he left his shift. Angry that he wasn't going to say goodbye.

But this kiss...

Anger dissipates as passion coils through me. I want the kiss. I want more than the kiss.

I want Luke. All of him.

So he's leaving to take care of an emergency. Wouldn't I do the same thing? He'll come back.

Back to me.

He deepens the kiss, a groan humming from him and into me. His chest, his abs, his shoulders—all beautifully light bronze, like a surfer god from LA. He could be a Renaissance statue. He pushes his erection against me.

And I don't want to run.

I never want to run from Luke. He's everything I want. Everything I need.

He rips his mouth from mine and meets my gaze, his brown eyes burning. "Tell me to stop," he says. "Tell me to stop now."

"I... I don't want you to stop."

"Please, Katelyn. Tell me. Because if you don't, I'm going to fuck you. I'm going to fuck you hard. No gentleness like the last time. I'm going to take you the way I want to take you. Like a wolf taking his mate. You're mine, Katelyn. Mine."

"Yours..."

"I'm not kidding." He cups my cheek. "I'm burning for you. And if you don't say no... If you don't leave right now—"

"Yes." The word comes out on a high breath. "Yes. Do it. Do it all. Please, Luke. All of it."

"Baby..."

"You don't have to be gentle with me. I've been through hell and back, but *back* is the operative word. I love you too, Luke, and I want to give you what you need. What we both need and want."

"I can't be gentle. Not this time. Not when I'm wanting you this badly."

"I'm not asking you to be. I'm just asking you to be Luke."

He narrows his eyes. "What if I'm *not* Luke?"

"Then be the wolf. I don't care. Be what you are in this moment."

"God, baby." His mouth comes down on mine once more, and he kisses me with desire, with passion, with an intoxicating intensity that's nearly as intimate as the act itself.

We kiss for several timeless moments, and I almost think

I could be satisfied with kisses alone...until he cups my breasts.

He breaks away from my mouth. "Take off that blouse, Katelyn."

"Don't you want to take it off for me?"

"If I take it off, it'll be in tatters."

God, those words. He's an animal. A beautiful, sexy animal. I want my blouse in tatters. I want him to rip every shred of clothing off me until there's nothing left but scraps and buttons.

I kick off my black pumps and stand in my bare feet.

But I make no move to remove my blouse.

"I'm warning you," he says, his voice dark and raspy. "I'll ruin it. I want to fucking ruin it, Katelyn."

Arrows shoot through my body, all landing in my pussy. God, my pussy. I'm slick already, soaking my panties.

"Do it," I say, only now realizing I'm speaking through clenched teeth. "Do it, Luke. Or whoever you are. Do it."

His hand is on the satin faster than lightning. He parts the shirt, and the pearl buttons go flying. He tugs it out of the waistband of my pants, turns me around, and pulls it off my arms.

I'm turned on, ready to—

"My God." His voice is different. "My God, Katelyn."

I turn. "What? What is it?"

"What the hell happened to you?"

My mouth drops.

Scars. Scars on my back. Mostly from Lovebird's beatings, but from other things as well.

"You know... You know my past."

"Baby. Oh my God." He turns me back around and gently

kisses along the scars. "Whoever did this to you should be shot."

"I won't argue."

He turns me back to face him. "I'm sorry. I'm sorry I said I couldn't be gentle."

"Luke, it's okay. I don't want you to be gentle. I want to feel every part of you, and I want you to make love the way you want to right now. And I—"

My gaze falls on his left arm.

The tattoo. Finally I can see the red and black image.

It's a raven—a black raven with a red eye, and it's wings... It's wings are made of fire. Black and red swirls float around it, drawn in such a way that I swear they're actually moving. The design drifts onto his shoulder, with swirls and flames dancing across his body.

"That's beautiful. Why are you having it removed?"

"I thought it didn't reflect who I am anymore," he says. "I was wrong."

I widen my eyes, part my lips.

"I thought I could leave it in the past."

"Your *past*?"

"Oh, baby. So much you don't know." He shakes his head. "You should go. Save yourself."

"What?"

"You heard me." His voice is harsh. Angry. "Get out. Leave."

I could easily obey. Leave. I don't have to bear whatever is troubling him. I have my own issues to deal with. Therapy. My new job that starts Monday.

All of which seems insignificant in the face of the man I love.

I gather my strength. "I'm not leaving. If you want me

gone, you'll have to physically remove me. Or call the police and report me for trespassing."

"Damn it, Katelyn. Please. I need you to leave."

"I'm absolutely not going to leave. I told you. You're going to have to physically remove me or have me removed."

"Fine. We'll do it your way." He stalks toward me and lifts me as if I weigh no more than a feather. He heads to the door, opens it.

I gasp. "I'm not wearing a shirt!"

He pauses, closes the door. Then he lets go of me. "Damn it, Katelyn. What am I going to do with you?"

I reach toward him, trail my fingers over his left arm, around the sharp lines of the raven's beak. "Fuck me. Like you said you would."

"You don't know what you're asking for." His eyes smolder.

"Luke, I'm not some untried child. I'm a woman. I'm nearly thirty years old."

"You've been through so much." He drops his head into his hands. "Those scars. I can't bear the thought."

"I've been through a lot." I touch his cheek. He's always so clean shaven. I wonder what his stubble might feel like beneath my fingertips? "And I think you have too."

"What I've been through is of no consequence. I made my own bed."

"Maybe, in some way, I did too."

He shakes his head vehemently and pushes my hand from his cheek. "You are not at all responsible for anything that happened to you. I don't ever want to hear you say that again."

"I suppose I didn't mean it that way. I know it wasn't my fault. It took me a long time during therapy to realize that.

What I meant was that it took me a while to find my strength. Even though it was with me all the time. There was a time when I begged Zee to end my life."

His eyes widen. "No…"

"It's okay. I'm not that woman anymore. I don't know what you're running from—and you *are* running—but I just want you to know that I want you. I need you. I love you. Please, don't leave me."

"Katelyn…" he growls.

"I meant what I said, Luke. Do it. Take me. Fuck me hard and fast. I can take it. I want it."

"At the risk of repeating myself, I don't think you know what you're asking for."

"At the risk of repeating *my*self, I'm a grown woman, and I'm saying yes. You told me before to leave. To leave or you would fuck me. I'm still here, Luke. I'm still standing. I think you *want* me to be scared of you or something."

"God, no."

"But you do. You're trying to scare me away because somewhere in your head you've decided that you're not good for me."

"I'm not."

"You've been a perfect gentleman with me. You haven't done anything without explicit permission. You *are* good for me, Luke. "

"I'm not who you think I am."

"And I'm not who you think *I* am. I'm not some fragile shell of a woman. I may not be quite myself, maybe not the person I was before those things happened to me, but I'm still whole. Whole in a different way. I want you. And I never imagined wanting a man like this. This is growth, Luke. Help me. Help me grow."

42

LUKE

She's so beautiful. So innocent. Oh, her body has been used in the worst way, but still she's innocent. Innocent in *my* eyes, and I don't want to taint her with the darkness that will always be with me. Not until I've redeemed myself. And for the first time, I believe that I may be able to. I believe that because she sees the good in me. She sees what I can be.

And I want to believe her. I so want to believe her.

I walk around her and regard the scars on her beautiful back. I have a few scars myself. One from a bullet, two from knives. None like this. I was never tortured. Never abused in the most heinous way. And although I did dole out my share of abuse, I never left a mark. Does that make me better than the men who abused Katelyn? Are there degrees of evil? Am I any different than those men on that treacherous island?

I sigh. Does it even matter? I did terrible things. Not just to women I thought I loved, but to friends, family. To my mother. My lovely mother who never stopped believing in me no matter what.

I trail my finger over one of Katelyn's scars. "Does it hurt?"

"Not anymore."

"I hate whoever did this to you. I wish I could kill them with my bare hands."

"It doesn't matter anymore."

"That man from the restaurant. Did he do this to you?"

She shakes her head.

"Who did, then? Who?"

"I couldn't tell you. They didn't use their real names. Most of them are in prison now. I'm not sure how Pollack isn't."

"He probably turned state's evidence." The thought makes me nauseous. I called Tony DeCarlo a canary when I saw him today.

The biggest canary is the one I see when I look in the mirror each morning.

But here stands Katelyn, knowing nothing about me and willing to let me take her. Ravage her. Do what I want with her. All because she loves me.

If only I were worthy...

I may never be, but I have to try.

I meant to leave. I meant to leave, to try to fix myself, and then come back to her.

But I know the truth.

And that truth is, once I go back, I may not get out of this alive.

Perhaps I will be worthy of her in the end, but it may be on my deathbed.

I am only a man. I'm not made of steel. Before me stands the woman I love—this beautiful scarred woman. I press my lips against one of her scars, and then I rain kisses across each one of them. "I love you, Katelyn. I love you. Scars and all."

She turns then, to face me, lifting her head to meet my gaze. "And I love you too, Luke. Scars and all."

I turn her around again and unclasp her bra, quickly removing it and tossing it to the floor.

Then I turn her to face me again. We're both naked from the waist up. She comes with her scars, I with mine.

I caress her shoulders, her upper arms, the tops of her breasts. Her nipples are pink and hard, and I bend down to take one between my lips.

"Oh..." A soft sigh escapes her throat.

My cock is hard. Hell, it's been hard since she came up here. I tried. I tried to get her to leave. I tried to get her to tell me no.

And now?

Now I'm going to take her. I'm going to fuck her, use her, ravage the hell out of her.

Love her.

Love her with everything I am, with everything I have and with everything inside my heart and inside my soul. As if it's the last time.

Because it very well may be.

I grab both of her breasts, palm them, squeeze them, and then I take her nipples between my thumbs and forefingers, twist them, pinch them softly.

A soft gasp leaves her throat.

"You like that?"

"My God, yes."

"These are mine. Mine, Katelyn. Your breasts are mine. Your body is mine. Your heart is mine."

"It's yours. All of it. And especially my heart."

I pinch her nipples harder, causing her to gasp again, and I meet her gaze. Wait for her to tell me to stop.

She doesn't.

I pinch them harder, harder, harder.

She groans, moving her hips, squeezing her legs together.

"Do you feel that emptiness in your soul?" I ask.

"Always. Always, except when I'm with you."

"I feel it too. Always, except when I'm with you. I want to take you. Fill you up. Stuff my cock into your pussy, make us one body, one heart, one soul."

Her cheeks grow pink at my graphic words, but she moans. A soft moan of contentment. She's eager. As eager as I am.

"I want to fuck you for hours," I say. "I want to make you come and come and come and come and come and come some more."

"And I..."

"What? What do you want, baby?"

"I want you to fuck me, Luke. And I want to fuck you. I want to suck your cock. I want to take your big hard dick between my lips and suck it all the way back to my throat."

I growl. A pure animal growl. It rumbles from my chest out my throat before I even know it's coming. This is Katelyn. My sweet Katelyn. She just talked dirty to me, and it is the hottest thing I've ever heard.

"We'll do it all," I tell her. "Everything you want and everything I want. I promise."

"Please..."

"You don't have to say please."

"I mean please... I need you...inside me. I want you too... I want to feel your mouth on me, Luke. I want to feel your tongue slide into me. I want so much. So much that I never experienced from someone I love and who loves me."

Her words strike me. Sadden me. All those times I've

done these things, and I truly thought I was loving the woman I was with. I know now that I was mistaking my need for control with love.

No more.

This time I know what love feels like, and I know how it feels to give it and to receive it.

"I'll do everything we both want," I promise. "I wish there were more hours in the day to love you."

"Luke, we have all the time in the world."

I don't reply. I don't tell her she's wrong. I don't tell her that once I go back to LA, my life is undoubtedly over. Instead I say nothing. I touch her cheek, thumb her beautiful lower lip.

Is there any harm in letting her think we have all the time in the world?

Probably, but I want her happy at this moment. I don't want anything tainting what is between us, at least not in her mind. Not yet.

I crush my mouth to hers, diving between her open lips with my tongue and taking her in a raw and passionate kiss. Our lips slide together as we both moan into each other's mouths. Kissing Katelyn... Nothing like it. Nothing like it in the world. It's like kissing a woman for the very first time and being kissed for the very first time. I could kiss her for hours. Kissing with her is almost as good as the entire act with anyone else.

But I don't have hours. She may think I do, but I don't.

Still... I give myself to the kiss. A few moments won't hurt. Won't matter. I'll still have time to take her, use her, love her in every way possible.

It is Katelyn who deepens the kiss. She presses her body

into mine, until we're as close together as we can possibly be. We kiss, and we kiss, and we kiss, until—

She trails her fingers over my arm, down to my hand, and places it between her legs.

She's still wearing her pants, but I rub the palm of my hand against her clit.

A soft moan escapes her, vibrates through her, and I swear I feel it against the palm of my hand.

I break the kiss. "Katelyn, tell me what you want."

"I already told you."

"Tell me again. Tell me what you want me to do to you."

"I want you to eat me." She giggles nervously, her cheeks and neck beautifully pink. The color travels to the tops of her breasts, and her nipples stick out like hard berries.

I rub against her softly. "I want to eat you. I want to slide my tongue up your pussy. I want to eat you till you scream. Until you're holding my hair and screaming in ecstasy."

"Please," she says. "All of that. *Please.*"

43

KATELYN

So safe. I feel so safe with Luke, in his arms. I'm asking for things I never dreamed I could put into words, but with Luke? He'll keep me safe.

He unclicks the snap on my pants, unzips the zipper slowly, brushes them down my ankles. I kick off my pumps, and step out of my pants, and now only my lace panties separate me from my heart's desire.

"You're so beautiful," Luke says. He touches between my legs, rubbing me through the thin fabric.

Already I know I'm soaked, and I know he feels the moistness. I wrap my arms around his neck. "Please…"

He kneels before me. Then he places his hands on my hips and slowly slides the panties over my thighs until they are on the floor. He touches his nose to my mound and inhales. "So sweet. You smell so sweet, Katelyn."

I close my eyes. I inhale, but of course I don't smell anything. At least I don't smell myself. Luke's smell permeates this apartment. His woodsy, piney smell.

"I love you," he says.

"I love you too." My eyes still closed.

I gasp then. His tongue is on my clit. Just gently, circling gently, but I'm ready to grab his hair with my hands and grind into him.

Before I have the chance, though he rises, turns me toward the bed, and gently lays me on it, my feet dangling over the side. Then he spreads my legs. "So beautiful." He breathes in.

Then his tongue is on me, and I grasp his bedspread in my fists. He licks me, explores me, gently and then not so gently. But all of it—every bit of it—is bringing me closer and closer and closer to the brink.

"I could eat you for hours," he says against my thigh before diving back in.

I've never experienced anything quite like this. Sure, I've had oral sex, although not a lot of it. Very little of it on the island, actually. Most of those men were eager to receive oral but not so eager to give it.

I wash the thought away from my mind. I don't want to poison this time with Luke.

He swirls his tongue over my clit, around my folds, and then pushes it inside me. I warm all over. My nipples are so hard, and my entire body is ready to erupt in flames.

"Please, Luke. Please..."

"Just tell me what you want, baby." He nips at my clit once more.

And that's all it takes. I shudder into an orgasm. An amazing and beautiful orgasm, and I open my eyes. I open my eyes and look into his while he's milking the orgasm out of me.

Ecstasy courses through me, but it's not enough. Never enough. I won't be truly full until he's inside me. Until we're joined as a couple, joined not only in body but in heart and soul.

I never believed in soulmates. Not even before the island, but I'm challenging that belief now. How else could Luke and I have fallen so quickly and so hard for each other?

"Come again," Luke commands. He dives back into my pussy, this time adding a finger, drilling into me and finding that elusive spot that I've heard of before but never experienced.

It's new. It's different. And it sends me reeling.

"That's it, baby. Come for me. I want you to come and come and come."

I close my eyes once more, as the pink cloud of passion envelops me, takes me higher and higher. Intensity rattles through me like a pinball, ricocheting here, there, and everywhere and then landing back between my legs.

He continues drilling his finger into me, continuous licking and sucking me, and I explode, again...again...again...

I ache to lift my hips, but with my dangling feet not touching the floor, I cannot. I do my best to grind into him, to show him how much he's pleasing me.

And he continues. He continues, and when I'm finally coming down from one more orgasm, he rips his mouth from my pussy and flips me over onto my stomach.

"Such a beautiful ass," he says. And then he slides his tongue between my cheeks.

I shudder. Shudder as if I'm alone in a cold forest. Except I'm not alone, and I'm not cold. I like what he's doing, which surprises me.

I erase all the images that want to come hurtling into my mind about how I've been violated in this place.

That's not me anymore. It will always be a part of me, but right now, right here, it has no bearing.

He ends up back at my pussy, though, perhaps sensing that I'm not ready to explore any back door activities. He sucks on me, bringing me to yet another orgasm, and—

The zing of his zipper, the rip of a condom packet—

And he's inside me. Finally. Easing that emptiness that has become a plague to my existence.

He thrusts hard. Hard. And then harder still.

No gentle love like that first time. He's making good on his promise to fuck me, and I'm loving it. Absolutely loving it.

I gasp with each thrust, but in a good way. I want him to take what he needs, and I want to always give it.

"God, Katelyn." He rams into me again and again.

"Luke! Luke, feels so good!"

"Yeah, baby. You like it? You like it when I fuck you?"

"God, yes." I grab the bedspread, pull it toward me, move my hips as best I can to meet his thrusts.

"Yeah, come on baby. Love this. Love you. God, have to come. I want to come inside you. Make you mine."

"I'm yours. Already yours, Luke."

And with those words from my lips, he pushes into me one last time, and he releases. So in tune to his body am I that I feel every contraction.

Mine. Mine. Mine. His voice with each pulse of his cock.

Mine. Mine. Mine. I say back to him.

And I know I'll never love this way again.

44

LUKE

Perfection.

I've now experienced complete perfection. Being one with Katelyn. It's so much more than sex, even more than making love.

It goes further than the ecstasy of the act, the passion of our love. It's the earth moving beneath us. Because of us.

I want to stay embedded inside her. Never leave this small apartment, this bed.

But I'm lost.

I withdraw from her, then head to the bathroom. I grab a clean washcloth out of my small cabinet, run it under the warm water of the sink, and then squeeze out the excess. I bring it to Katelyn, who has rolled over onto her back. A lovely pink flush covers her body, and her nipples, though no longer rigidly hard, stand out against her areolas. She looks like an artist's watercolor. So beautiful.

I gently clean her.

"That feels nice."

I regard her. This is the first time I've truly looked at her naked. I stand before her the same way, and as I'm thinking that very thought, she opens her eyes.

I follow her gaze as it meanders up and down my body. She seems to pay close attention to my left arm and shoulder, but she zeroes in on something other than the tattoo.

"You were shot," she says.

"Yes."

"Who shot you?"

I don't like to think about it. I deserved to be shot. I was trying to take a woman against her will. Not unlike Katelyn had been taken.

I didn't commit the horrors that the men who visited Katelyn on the island did, but I committed my own kind of horrors against my last girlfriend. I kept her captive, told her she couldn't leave, locked her in. When I had way too much to drink, I even sometimes struck her.

All of these reasons...

All of these reasons are why I do not deserve Katelyn now.

The only way I may come close to deserving her is if I go back. If I go back and face what I've done and make amends as best I can.

And if I go back...

I may lose my life.

But I have to do it. Katelyn could make me happy, but she has to know who I am. Perhaps I could have dealt with this—perhaps I could have truly become Luke Johnson—if I never met Katelyn.

But I did.

And she, along with the trip to visit Anthony DeCarlo, made me see the light.

I was not born to be every man and no man. I was born to be me.

Lucifer Charles Ashton III.

Named for the devil I became.

Street name—Lucifer Raven. Sometimes called simply The Raven.

Son of multimillionaire producer Lucifer Charles Ashton Junior and his wife, my mother. Charmaine Louise Portugal Ashton.

The woman who never gave up on me, even when I gave up on myself.

So I'll go back. Back to LA. Back to the drug lords who want me dead. And back to my old man, who though he has no love lost for me, bailed me out with his money.

Luke Johnson is my own creation. Though I had help from my one FBI contact, I'm not in the Witness Protection Program. I did this on my own with my father's help. After I gave up evidence to put several kingpins away.

I got immunity for my efforts as long as I went into rehab and therapy.

I did well. I understand now why I was wrong, and I understand how the alcohol played a part in my actions.

But my actions, alcohol or not, are my own.

I own them.

I'll never take another drink, no matter how much a glass of wine or bourbon calls to me.

I've been here in Manhattan for a while now, working at The Glass House. Never once have I taken a drink.

I absolutely won't. It's nonnegotiable.

"You are a beautiful man, Luke," Katelyn says.

"Not nearly as beautiful as you are." I join her on the bed and take her into my arms.

Our lips meet, in a ravenous and hungry kiss. I need more of her. I will need it, to get through what is to come.

I move from her lips to her neck to her ear. "I'm going to love you again," I whisper to her.

She shudders against me.

"I'm going to love you again and again."

I roll over so that I'm on top of her, holding my weight on my arm so as not to crush her. I look into her sparkling blue eyes and I see her love reflected back at me.

This is it.

This may be the last time I make love with Katelyn.

And I'm going to make it count.

I meld our mouths together, slide our lips together, swirl my tongue around hers. It's a long and hungry kiss, and my cock is hard and ready to go again.

She pulls me toward her and then maneuvers her body somehow so that we're back on our sides. I break the kiss and lift my eyebrows.

"I want to give you what you've given me," she says.

"You are."

"No. You went down on me. I want to do the same for you."

My cock hardens even further. I don't hate the idea. I love the idea, in fact. But is Katelyn ready to do that?

She feels she is, so who am I to second-guess her? This may be the last time I'm with her, so I don't want to let her down. And damn, I want those ruby red lips around my dick.

"Oh, baby. Please…"

45

KATELYN

I never imagined wanting to do this for any man. Not after what I've been through. But Luke—while he hasn't made me forget the past, he makes me want to experience these things the way they were supposed to be experienced.

He's large. Really large. After so many years of hating the sight of a man's naked body, of having it used as a weapon against me, now I find myself aching for it.

For this particular man.

I gather my courage and reach forward to touch him. It's hard, of course—hot and hard, though the skin covering it is smooth like satin.

How different it feels to want to touch it. Because I love the man it's attached to.

I trail my fingers along its length, and then over the silky head. A clear drop of liquid emerges, and Luke groans.

"My God, baby. What you do to me."

"You're beautiful," I say, and I realize I'm telling the

unadulterated truth. Every part of him is beautiful, even this part—this part that, on other men, was used to harm me.

But not by Luke.

Never by Luke.

Our first time was so gentle. And while this time wasn't, he made sure I knew at the outset what I was in for, and he gave me the choice to walk away.

I roll my finger over the curve of the head, touching the drop of liquid and massaging it into his tip.

He sucks in a breath. "Baby, please..."

"Tell me how to please you," I say. "I want to please you so badly."

"You *are* pleasing me. I don't want to tell you what to do. I want you to do what you feel comfortable with."

I gaze into his eyes. I see love there, and I see promise. Most of all I see the truth. He's speaking the truth. I'm no innocent, obviously. I know how much men like getting head, and I know that this gentle touching of my hands is probably just driving him insane.

But still, he's letting me go at my own pace.

And because of that, I want to please him all the more.

I touch my tongue to the tip of his dick and lick off the pearl of salty liquid.

He sucks in another breath.

His body goes rigid, his arms straighten at his side.

I meet his gaze. "Tell me. I want to please you. I want you to do what feels right. Do you want to touch me? Touch my head? Force me down on it? It's okay. I want you to be pleased."

He groans again. "You're so beautiful, Katelyn, and I'm not talking about the outside right now. You're beautiful on the inside. You have such a big heart, and it kills me to know..."

He closes his eyes. "I can't do this. I can't do it." He scoots away from me on the bed.

"Luke?"

"I don't deserve you."

"What's this about? Of course you deserve me. I'm the one who doesn't deserve you."

"How can you say that?"

"Because... Because I'm...soiled. I'll never be the woman you deserve."

"Oh my God. That can't be how you see yourself."

"It's...not. I mean not really. I've been through the therapy. I know none of it was my fault. But sometimes..."

He touches my cheek. "I understand. Sometimes what other people say doesn't change something you feel in the marrow of your bones."

"Yes. That's it exactly. How do you understand so well?"

"I have a past too, Katelyn, and it's not pretty. If I were any kind of a man, I would never have come near you in the first place."

"I promise you it won't make a difference to me."

He closes his eyes. Then he sighs. A long and drawn-out sigh, and with it I hope comes some healing power.

But then he opens his eyes. I'm not sure what I see in them. They're wide, and he's almost glaring at me.

"Luke?"

"I want a drink."

"No. Don't."

"I don't have anything in the house. But I need something."

"Please. Don't undo what you've done. You've come so far."

He nods. Then he closes his eyes, and when he opens them once more, he's the Luke I know.

I move toward him once more, lick the tip of him gently.

But he moves away again.

"Luke, I want to—"

"I want it to, Katelyn. You have no idea how much I want it. I'm not made of steel. I'm a man just like every other man, and I love you. I want you to suck me."

"Then let me. I'm right here."

"I can't. Not yet." He pulls me into his arms. "Just lie with me. Please. I want to hold you in my arms, feel you next to me. I want to inhale the sweet scent of your hair, kiss those beautiful lips."

"All right," I say, trying to keep the disappointment out of my voice. "If that's what you want."

"It's what I know is right. At this moment."

I snuggle into his shoulder then. I inhale his musky scent, kiss his chest, and then close my eyes."

~

I JERK AWAKE. The room is dark, and for a moment a sharp spike of fear slides through me. I don't know where I am—

I heave a sigh of relief when I realize I'm still at Luke's apartment. I remember falling asleep in his arms, feeling so safe and secure.

I reach toward him, and—

Where is he?

Probably in the bathroom. I look toward the door leading to the bathroom, but there's no sliver of light at the bottom. He probably just got up to go and didn't bother with the lights. Didn't want to wake me.

I draw in a deep breath, stretch my arms above my head. Relaxation swirls through me, and I close my eyes. I imagine myself lying on a beach, the sun streaming down on me, warming my body and my soul. In the distance the waves crash, and I feel at home.

So at home here with Luke.

Soon I'm asleep again.

46

LUKE

The bus station is eerily quiet at three in the morning. I didn't think anyone in Manhattan ever slept. I'm not looking forward to a cross-country bus ride, but I'll be able to keep much more under the radar than if I tried flying or renting a car.

I bought my ticket with cash, and now I wait.

Until—

Something nudges the small of my back.

"Where the hell do you think you're going?" a deep voice says.

"Who the hell are you?" I begin to look over my shoulder but—

Fuck. It's a gun. It nudges harder into my back.

"You really didn't think you could hide from us, did you?"

"I don't know what you're talking about," I say, willing my voice not to crack.

I can handle whoever this is. I've handled worse.

Of course... When I had to handle worse, I wasn't a fucking stool pigeon.

"I think you know where this ends," the voice says.

"We'll see where it ends." I scan the station.

I see one security guard. Just one. No police officers.

I'm not sure how I can get the security guard's attention. I'm not sure if I even want to. Whoever this is, if he's anything like I used to be, he's already taken care of the security guard.

"What the fuck do you want?" I say through gritted teeth.

"Not much," he says. "Just your big head on a fucking silver platter...*Lucifer Raven.*"

LUKE AND KATELYN'S story concludes in *Raven*, coming January 25, 2022!

A NOTE FROM HELEN

Dear Reader,

Thank you for reading *Moonstone*. If you want to find out about my current backlist and future releases, please visit my website, like my Facebook page, and join my mailing list. If you're a fan, please join my street team to help spread the word about my books. I regularly do awesome giveaways for my street team members.

If you enjoyed the story, please take the time to leave a review. I welcome all feedback.

I wish you all the best!

Helen

http://www.helenhardt.com/signup

ACKNOWLEDGMENTS

Thank you so much to the following individuals who helped make *Moonstone* shine: Karen Aguilera, Linda Pantlin Dunn, Serena Drummond, Christie Hartman, Kim Killion, and Angela Tyler.

ABOUT THE AUTHOR

#1 *New York Times*, #1 *USA Today*, and #1 *Wall Street Journal* bestselling author Helen Hardt's passion for the written word began with the books her mother read to her at bedtime. She wrote her first story at age six and hasn't stopped since. In addition to being an award-winning author of romantic fiction, she's a mother, an attorney, a black belt in Taekwondo, a grammar geek, an appreciator of fine red wine, and a lover of Ben and Jerry's ice cream. She writes from her home in Colorado, where she lives with her family. Helen loves to hear from readers.

Please sign up for her newsletter here:
http://www.helenhardt.com/signup
Visit her here:
http://www.helenhardt.com

CPSIA information can be obtained
at www.ICGtesting.com
Printed in the USA
LVHW110835231021
701184LV00033B/166